MW01282285

I'M ONLY
HUMAN
AFTER ALL

ALEX I. ROGERS

ISBN: 1461051916

ISBN-13: 9781461051916

FOREWORD

THIS BOOK IS THE FIRST in a series of three coming-of-age books that are based on my life. *I'm Only Human After All* is the story of my early adolescent life and the issues that all of us can relate to at that stage in our lives. At some time we have all been in an awkward stage until, one day, we surface as something more. We were all once awkward kids trying to find our way. This is just the prologue of how I found my way into adulthood. I feel that the events described in this book are relatable to all of us, in one way or another, at some point in our lives. In this book I expose and deal with a large number of issues, such as finding my identity, dealing with sibling rivalry, realizing my self-worth, trust, betrayal, acceptance, bullying, and much more. If I could label a central theme of this work, I would identify it as "bullying." Most of this story follows my personal experiences with both bullying and cyber-bullying and their effects on me. Just for the record, I would like to state that bullying in any shape or form is wrong, and everyone should be treated with equal respect. In my life I have come to understand that all people should be treated as equal, and if we are to move positively in any emotion, it should be in love.

My ultimate goal for this series is that when people read it, they can learn and grow from it. While I briefly gave you a small outline of the story regarding themes, hidden truths are scattered all throughout this book. I hope that after reading this book you part with something that you didn't have before, something that will stay with you and grow into something more.

Happy reading,
ALEX I. ROGERS

CHAPTER 1

HOW IT ALL STARTED

M Y ALARM RANG. Even in a dream state, I knew what that meant. It meant that it was seven o'clock sharp. I swatted at the alarm out of desperation for it to stop ringing, but it was no use. I had to get up. It was Tuesday morning, and my obligation as a minor was to get ready for school. As I brought myself to face the day, I stumbled though a swamp of dirty laundry that was left on my floor from days past. I literally had to high step through it all to get to the other side of the room. Traversing through the field of dirty laundry, I stumbled upon the treasure I had been searching for all along; a green shirt and ruffled khakis were lying between my feet. It was my uniform for school that I had on the day before. I bent over and smelled them…nothing odd lashed out at me, so I deemed them good to go.

I got dressed in a hurry. I always did. After putting the finishing touches on my uniform, I glanced at the clock.

It was only seven fifteen, and I was fully dressed, sans the non-essentials. I skipped out on brushing my teeth and combing my hair. Dad would be furious if he saw me like this, but it wasn't like I was trying to impress anybody or anything…besides, school started at eight. I was going to be late if I took time to do the little things. It wasn't going to kill me if I had nappy hair for a day. I had to leave now if I wanted to make it on time. As I heard the thunder outside the house, I realized that it would take even more time to get where I needed to be. Just by the silence of the house, I could tell the others had already left. This was a bad omen. You see, on an average day, I was the first one out of the house besides Dad.

With this in mind, I grabbed a piece of toast and stuck it in my mouth as I rushed out of the house. It wasn't long before I spat it out. Just that quick I had forgotten it was raining…I didn't know how I'd forgotten, though. Mom told me at least a thousand times since Sunday that the forecast was scattered thunderstorms for the whole week. This was an awful way to remember; weather is so crazy in Louisiana.

By the time I was halfway down the block, my saturated clothes were already beginning to weigh me down; by the time I was at the school grounds, I was barely able to move. The cars seemed to be doing just fine though. They were all lined up near the entrance of the school. It was the drop-off line.

For some reason the sight struck me differently today. All of those people in their cars had their own story to tell. It's common sense, but a lot of people don't pick up on it…well, it's better to say that a lot of people choose to ignore it. Somehow, though, in the process of life, we get the notion that we're not important, that we're irrelevant to the big picture. If I were to ask anyone in those cars, "What are your hopes, your dreams, your ambitions?" would they be able to answer? Too many people just go through life going through the motions…you're not alive if you've never done anything worth sharing. You've never lived if you never fought for something you believed in. So many people die with their dreams in their hands and it scares me. But why?

∽

In my younger days, I tried to listen to those whose song had enticed me, but those were usually the ones who were shunned by the rest. I remember my first best friend, Ross. My mom always said he was *off,* but I didn't notice. Maybe it was because I was quite off myself; I was only eight at the time. Ross and I would fantasize about cartoons and video games throughout most of our second-grade lives. We talked about it so much that we even decided to make up our own. Even at a young age, we put countless hours into making our dream a reality. It's amazing that we even passed the second grade.

By the end of the school year, we even had a full script. I didn't realize it at the time, but we had done a powerful thing. We'd done something at a young age that many, even in their latter years, have never set out to do. We followed our dream and did exactly what we wanted to do. And we were proud…we had reason to be. The feelings must have been equivalent to how God felt when he created the Heavens and the Earth. I remember feeling the finished product in my hands, and all I could think of was, "It was good," and it was perfect in my sight. It was made in my image, crafted by "the master" for my own purpose. I thought of it as my masterpiece and bragged about it whenever a situation arose that allowed me to talk about it—and even sometimes when it didn't. Creation is a powerful thing; the ability to create what you desire is only limited by what you can think of. That was what I took from it; Ross, on the other hand, took things a little bit too far.

"Legend of Kajaita" was the name of the game, which had twenty-four characters. I don't remember them all, but I'm pretty sure that's the number. When Ross and I finished the game script, we took two different roads. While I was content with my accomplishments, Ross was becoming more and more obsessed with his. While we both controlled the characters, he took a special liking toward the ones that he had priority over. For whole school days, he would act out his characters and religiously quote lines from the script, and that drew attention—and I'm not talking about the good kind. Because of his new-found adoration, the kids began to shun him, while I continued to progress socially.

Now that I think about it, some people refused to be my friend, just because I was Ross's friend. Kids can be so cruel...he was just into his work. It didn't bother me, but the other kids made fun of him, regardless. I haven't talked to him in years...I seriously need to catch up with him.

Thinking back on past times isn't exactly my favorite thing to do. Not to be a downer or anything, it's just that I tend to think of the what-ifs, the could-have-beens, and the if-onlies. Especially in my younger years; for instance, my first crush in middle school.

Her name was Miranda Thompson. She was the daughter of a teacher at our school. For a fourteen-year-old she had a lot of spunk at the time—quite feisty, actually. She was quite the charmer. Maybe it was her charisma. Even at that age, it seemed the world was her stage…kudos to her. On the other hand, at fourteen, I wasn't exactly the most polished shoe in the closet. Matter of fact I was like the weird one of the class—OK, more like the outcast.

But still, I regret that I never took that chance. In life chances only happen once. What's that famous saying again? I think it goes, "Opportunity only strikes once… and if you don't act, you can only watch it pass you by." She was beautiful too. She had caramel-smooth skin, and her eyes reminded me of pure jade. In after-school care, I'd always be on the team against her and play four-square. She was like my rival, although it was an innocent rivalry. I remember how after our games we would just sit and talk about nothing till my mom picked me up at about six. It was nice, but no matter how much we got along, "connected" or whatever, I never really had the chance to tell her that I liked her. It wasn't as if had I told her, things would get super serious. We were only fourteen (if that)…and it's not like when I'm just sitting here I reflect on what could have been between us. That's just weird. I don't know…it's just that she kind of represents something to me. I'm not sure what, but she just does. I'm still working on it.

Now that I think of it, everyone that I knew from my middle school still has a piece of my heart, even though those days are long gone. In the end it turned out OK, I guess. Some of them from my old school actually go here with me now.

❦

I kept on walking through the wet lot and on inside the school's main building. Upon entering, I looked up at a clock on the wall. I had about fifteen minutes till the bell rang. It was sad though; usually I'd sit outside and enjoy the break unit it was time for class to start. Today I would have to improvise, it seemed. Looking outside I realized that the rain had gotten even worse compared to when I first left the house. I was in a bit of luck, though, because I spotted one of my friends farther up the hall by his locker. He was hunched over, stuffing his bag with books for the classes ahead. Without hesitation I waved him down and approached him.

"Hey! What's up?"

He looked up and stood. We were only inches apart now, and he was reminiscent of a mountain. I had seen him the day before, but just to say hi and bye. But standing this close to him really brought his height into perspective. Devan was always big for his age, but over the summer he had really shot up. Now he had to be at least a foot taller than me.

He let out a sigh and tilted his head against the locker.

"Nothing much, man."

"Classes stressing you out already?" I asked. "It's only day two...it can't be that bad."

"I know, man, but I'm getting tired of all this school..."

"You've grown so much over the summer, you might be able to quit and play basketball. You're like the Jolly Green Giant, except you're black."

"Funny...and you're like the only black kid I know with freckles, so we're even."

"I'm serious...you know I actually have to look up at you for us to have a conversation."

"Ha-ha, and you seriously resemble a plump chocolate chip cookie but whatever, man...I'm not judging. So what you up to now?"

"Nothing. Just thought I'd swing by and say hello. Not that much going on…and I don't think it's going to get any better with all that rain outside."

"Yeah, it ain't looking too great out there…and there's nothing much to say about being in here either."

"Yeah…new school, but it's cool though, right? I mean we're just freshman, so this is like a new chapter in our lives. Pretty soon we'll be up there in the ranks. You just got to tough it out. By the time we're sophomores, we'll have our fair share of crazy stories to tell and a bunch of friends to go with it."

"I guess...you're way too optimistic, Mr. Rogers."

He said that with a blank expression. Pretty much the whole conversation we had he was like that. I didn't want to admit it, but I knew what was bothering him. Before we graduated from middle school, our teacher took the time to sit us down and break us in to what awaited us. Looking back I guess she had to do it. We were pretty naïve. Our school was small, and our graduating class was only thirty-two students. But she could have gone about it in a tamer manner. You see, Devan didn't rank that high in the class. He struggled on conventional tests.

"OK class, I'm going to be frank," our teacher had said. "If you guys have been going here all your lives, chances are you're sheltered. Now for the most part, that's all of you. So, this is going to be tough." She pulled down something from the projector. "These are the average statistics of middle school students moving into high school. More specifically, it shows the potential reasons for dropouts.

Out of all the girls in the room, half will become pregnant and drop out. One-fourth of you will not have the academic aptitude to make it past junior year…even fewer for college." She went on. "This is a penis…" and on. "This is a vagina…" and on. "Remember 'no' means 'NO!'" But as she spoke, one thing really caught my attention. "Class, I want you to know…things are going to be different from this point on. You're in eighth grade, so you're the big dogs at this school, but when you get to high school, you'll be at the bottom of the totem pole."

For the next couple of days after she said that, it continued to echo in my head. I'd forgotten how it felt to be at the bottom, because during my time in middle school, I had made it to the top. After graduation from middle school, the thought had left my head, but seeing Devan worried like that caused me to entertain the thought.

"Hey, I'm going to go to class. The bell's going to ring in a bit…see ya," Devan said.

"OK."

He picked up his bags and walked off to his next class. I figured I should do the same. The bell was about to ring, after all. As I walked down the halls, I tapped my pencil on my chin and thought, *Bottom of the totem pole, eh?*

The bell rang.

The thought of being on the bottom again danced around my head on the way to class. It even lingered once it started. I simply couldn't shake the thought. I even began sketching out the concept on my desk with the eraser side of my pencil. In the end I only came up with one conclusion.

If this is the bottom, it sure doesn't feel like it…it's all about perception.

Throughout the rest of the day, the same thought managed to weave itself in and out of my consciousness. I thought I had solved it earlier, but my mind said otherwise.

New beginnings always had something special—starting at the bottom and making it to the top produced something magical. When you reach your destination, your goal, that's when it really hits home. Maybe that's why I felt the way I did. I knew I was just a kid, but eventually I'd become something much more. Eventually I'd be at the top.

Someday.

CHAPTER 2

THE CLIMB

THE NEXT FEW DAYS went by quickly. Everything was going smoothly. I finally adjusted to my teachers and schedule, and I was starting to get the hang of this whole high school thing. I now had the time to make new friends. It was something I had been neglecting up until this point—sadly. That's why this morning I sprung out of bed and raced to school. On my way Devan crossed my mind. In the past couple of days, I really hadn't heard much from him. We needed to catch up. I'd feel pretty bad if I left him for some other friends I'd just met…he'd been with me ever since middle school. I couldn't allow that to happen, so I decided to make it top priority to eye him out.

When I got there, he wasn't in his usual spot, but it didn't take me long to find him. He was in a corner with some new friends of his, a pair I'd seen before. They were both lanky and slightly built. The only difference was their height and facial features. Either way you put it, they resembled talking dark skeletons. The taller one was named

Rasheed and the shorter, Sheldon. They both sat behind me in history class, and both of them were active in sports. Rasheed was on the football team and Sheldon played basketball. Out of the two, Rasheed was pretty much the leader. Sheldon was only there for the occasional co-sign. The only thing I would hear from them in class was how stupid the teacher was and other obnoxious comments. Typical jock behavior. I really didn't have anything against them; I just wished they would be quiet in class, that's all. The most the teachers would ever do was tell them to be quiet... if that. Other than that I steered clear of anything that involved them. As I walked down the hall toward Devan, he looked at me with a cold stare.

He was surprised to see me for some reason. I mean, I knew it had been awhile but sheesh. "Hey, Devan, what's up?" I asked. "Haven't seen you all week." At that moment I threw out my hand expecting him to dap me off, but he didn't respond. Instead, Rasheed bitterly batted my hand down with his boney hands and looked over at Devan.

"You know this kid?"

I looked at the three of them, eager for his response.

"No," he said. "He won't stop following me...I think he's gay."

"Devan..."

The short one nudged him.

"Now that you mention it, he does look kinda homo."

At that moment I felt a mix of confusion and pain. I couldn't even fathom that this was really happening. As I looked at Devan, I could feel the remorse oozing from him. But still, regardless of how he felt, he still betrayed me and retained his resentment. I didn't know how to react. I couldn't even see a motive behind his actions. Maybe the measure of our friendship wasn't as strong as I had thought it out to be. The only friend I had abandoned me for people he had just met. The irony. Not only that, but in the process, he'd spit on my name...and on me.

At that moment we broke eye contact. I knew how he felt from looking at him. But could he feel the pain I felt by looking at me? Was this the extent of our friendship? The first week of high school? I wanted to scream at him to look at me, but he couldn't. He wouldn't. Of course he couldn't. You can never look someone in the eye after you've back-stabbed them because you know that you're the sole reason for their pain.

As I stood there, the other two went back and forth, analyzing me, critiquing me, ripping me head to toe; but to me that was all in the distance. Irrelevant. My sights were set on Devan. Everything else was just white noise. I knew what had happened, but I refused to accept it. I was in shock. It didn't bother me that I had two vultures picking at my corpse, my very essence. My shock quickly turned into rage and then to uncertainty; my heart began to race even faster. I wanted to react, but I didn't know how. By the time I had gathered the strength to say what was on my mind, they had already vanished; just as quickly as it started, it ended. Before I even knew what happened, the three of them walked away. And why wouldn't they? The damage had already been done. A rotting corpse lay in the hallway to show it. A mere decomposing body left in the wind.

For the next few days, I felt like I was just going through the motions. By morning I sulked, and by night I was af-flicted. My mind was plagued with questions. Was this my fault? What's wrong with me? Was he really even my friend in the first place? I had fallen into darkness, and I had to climb my way out.

This must have been what our teacher was telling us about. The bottom is a hard place to be. Devan realized that, so he found a quick way to boost himself up, but in the process he pulled me down. And the funny thing was, we weren't really doing that badly until now.

Crabs in a barrel…that's the only way I can describe it. Have you ever seen a bunch of crabs in a barrel? All of them are trying to escape and make it to the top so what happens is they climb by bringing the other crabs down. In the end it's a futile struggle because every crab is pulling a different crab. If anything they end up in a worse position then they started in because they are ensnared on both ends. Devan, in his stupidity, chose this route.

I mean, we weren't popular, but we weren't outcasts either. But now I had this to deal with. If he wanted to make new friends, fine, congratulations, but this wasn't the way to do it. Throwing me, an innocent bystander, into the mix was foul play. It didn't take a genius to know that nothing good could come from this. So if you were wondering if the grass is greener on the other side…it's not.

With everything going on, the weekend flew by. I found myself lying in my bed thinking about what the day held for me. As I lay there, I tried to bring myself to move, but my body ached. I could feel something lingering in my chest, griping me, holding me back. I was still feeling oppressed from what had happened last Friday. Being around family helped, but the bad feeling kept finding a way to creep back into my psyche. I was amazed how much emotional distress could affect the body. I tried once more and was finally able to convince myself to move out of bed. It was at a slower pace than usual. The world was still more or less a blur around me. Somehow, I ended up at school.

On the campus I couldn't help but notice a tall statue in the middle of the grounds. The reality of being a high school student was still setting in. This was the high school experience, and therefore, a new chapter in my life. It was OK to get knocked down as long as you got back up. I promised myself that day that I wouldn't be defeated. I might fall sometimes, but I'd always come back stronger. This was all just one big mountain. Life was just one big mountain, and it was also something that I had to climb.

With that being said, I approached the entrance to the main building with a deep breath and gripped the door handle. I exhaled as I swung the door open.

Nothing.

Everything was as if nothing had happened. But then, again, I didn't see anyone that knew me. I made my way to my locker and began to pack my books. From the corner of my eye, I saw Rasheed and Sheldon approach me. I pretended to ignore them, but they still circled me like I was their prey. I didn't look at them directly. I was still packing, but I could feel them scanning me up and down, sizing me up. I felt like I was about to be their next meal. Bloodlust was written all over their salivating faces. It was clear that they had bad intentions. They were out to eat me alive, consume my pride, and destroy my dignity.

Rasheed pushed my locked door closed.

"Hey, faggot."

I never understood bullying or the whole dominance thing. Why couldn't he just let me be? Was it really that much of a kick to make people feel lesser than you? If so,

I wouldn't give him the pleasure. Maybe if I ignored him, he would leave me alone.

Since he had taken the liberty of closing my locker door for me, I told him thank you as I put my books in my bag and began to walk away. I could feel the tension clawing at my back as I inched away from him. Two things were on my mind at the time: don't look back and don't say a word. I just kept repeating those words over and over in my head and kept walking. My feet grew heavy with the rising tension. It felt like the whole hall was a gravity well. The hallway was heavy, as well; just taking ten steps felt like I was midway through a trek across the Sahara. As I walked away from him, I could feel his eyes burning a hole into my skull. In the midst of it all, things were going pretty good though.

Yes, I had a crazy guy behind me trying to kill me, but at the same time, I had avoided a major conflict. Because I diffused the situation quickly, no one had seen what had happened. But I knew this was far from over. I had embarrassed him in front of his right-hand man. It made him look weak. His ego was bruised. He probably felt humiliated. His next course of action was most likely going to be payback, and judging by how mad he was, it would probably come with interest.

Whatever…I swear there was an invisible pecking order at school. It wasn't right and it didn't justify things like this. Playing a sport or being a member of whatever didn't make the world your playground. It was unwise to play with people's emotions. We all deserved respect.

Who did he think he was to take mine away from me? Did he think I was just going to sit down and let someone walk all over me…it's funny, there was actually a time where someone had literally walked all over me.

When I was younger, my cousin Ron and I used to get picked on in elementary school. We were young so, of course, our parents got involved, but instead of going to the principal, they went to my renegade aunt, Aunt Jackie.

Aunt Jackie, come to think of it, was more of a drill sergeant than an aunt. She would always push us to do more…even if her methods were unconventional. When a problem came up that my parents didn't quite know how to handle, they went over to see Aunt Jackie; when they had a problem with me, they went over to see Aunt Jackie; when they had a problem with someone else, they went over to see Aunt Jackie. For anything that couldn't be solved with conventional knowledge, we pretty much went to see Aunt Jackie.

I can say now that I've had my fair share of Aunt Jackie's drill sessions to last me a lifetime, but I'll probably end up in another one before I know it. Over the summers when I was younger, we used to stay at my grandma's house during the day. Our dad would drop off my two brothers and me at her house in the morning and come back to get us around dinner when he got off work. In that time frame, from the moment we set foot in that house to the moment we left, we were under Jackie's rule, which was a good thing: she toughened us up.

Yes, she chewed me out countless times over not making up my bed or not cleaning the dishes. I hate to say it, but she did build character…boy did she build character. I remember when she chewed me out about letting kids walk all over me in school during recess, and you know what she did? She literally walked all over me. She told me to lie down my back and said, "I'm going to show you how it feels to have someone walk all over you," and she actually did it. Then she called me "doormat," until I learned how to stick up for myself. What an aunt, eh? Anyway, I have a lot to thank her for…even if she was a little bit crazy.

With her unorthodox training under my belt, it was possible to turn my back to Rasheed and Sheldon and walk the remainder of the hall. It was a relief. I had left the building in one piece. In a fight the worst thing you can possibly do is turn your back on an opponent. It wasn't the brightest choice I made, but it had to be done. I wasn't going to stoop to their level.

It still bugged me, though, that he went to such lengths to make my life miserable. I just didn't get it…I probably never would. It was weird how people actually got off on that. Maybe I was just different. I mean, if I were gay, then it would make him look even worse. Because of my sexual orientation, he would take it upon himself to mentally, physically, and verbally abuse me. Not to "set me straight" but for his own enjoyment…I just couldn't get his mindset. Because I was different, I was therefore considered less than him? I just didn't get it. Discrimination in a nutshell.

I guess that some people are really lost.

The rest of the day went smoothly. I didn't have another run-in with Sheldon, Rasheed, or Devan, so pretty much everything was good. Actually, the rest of the week sailed through rather smoothly. That last little standoff seemed to have done the trick.

The weekend was good too; I had a chance to catch up on my rest and relaxation. I even put in a few extra hours into studying. I never really realized it, but being at home was like a safe haven. When I was there, I felt that nothing could go wrong. I guess I came out lucky in that department. My whole family was together. My father and mother had been happily married for sixteen years, and I had two brothers, an older one, Jason, and a younger one, Craig. My family had always been there for me, but at times I found myself especially thankful for my father.

My dad never knew his father, so instead he was raised by his mom, along with his grandpa and grandma. Sadly, all three of them passed away within a short span of time. The thing I marveled at about him was that, through all of this, he didn't use his anger and grief as an excuse to turn away from what he believed in. The average person would have caved under the heartbreak and called it quits, but my dad still moved on. During all this he was still head over the youth group and ministries at his local assembly and was a full-time student. Even after his girlfriend of three years left him in college, he still never gave in to his suffering. He said that God kept him through his suffering, so when he got older, he decided to do for others as God had done for him.

He became a pastor and eventually built his own church. The love and passion that he showed when operating in the church, he showed at home. Our home was never a place that I dreaded coming to, and our guests felt the same way. We would have countless visitors every week that came to seek guidance for their lives. Whether it was marriage counseling, self-help, or just someone to lean on, my dad was there. When I was younger, I used to sit there and think, *Wow, this is my dad…and I don't even have to do anything to get him.* Now, years later, that thought still sticks with me, but I've come to terms with it. He is my one and only dad, and there couldn't be a better one.

It was Monday again. Even though I was feeling refreshed, school was the last thing I wanted to do, especially after coming back from the weekend. Now I know why people hate Mondays. I sluggishly pulled myself from my bed and got dressed. I actually took my time today when leaving the house. For some reason I just felt like taking things slowly. As I got dressed, it dawned on me that it was one of those days where you can live life for what it was.

Yeah, it was a calm, quiet morning, until I heard my mom thrashing in the hallway. I peeped out my door and found clothes scattered everywhere. Mom was getting ready for work. Without realizing it I had gotten up early.

Watching her get ready was like watching a tornado touch down. All she left was destruction in her wake. She spared no one. If you needed the bathroom, she had it first. If you were in the bathroom, she kicked you out. She took no prisoners when it came to getting ready for work…it was best to avoid her during her morning rush.

On the way downstairs, I popped in her doorway and gave her a quick "good morning." She signaled back to me, waving her curling iron in her hair. When I got to the kitchen, I saw that nothing was out yet, so I decided to give it a shot and make my own feast. When it came to cooking, I was really not the best out there, but I was pretty sure I could hold my own.

I began my mission to prepare breakfast for myself. I searched around the pantry for the supplies I needed. I decided to give waffles a try. I seriously don't get the difference between pancakes and waffles besides the obvious. When it comes down to it, it's still just fried bread. So it couldn't be that hard; besides, I had directions.

Materials needed: 3 eggs, ½ tsp. of salt, 1 tsp. of baking soda, 2 tsp. of baking powder, ¾ cups of flour, ½ cups of butter milk, and 1 stick of butter.

- **Step one: Gather eggs and mix them into a medium size bowl.**
- **Step two: Add flour, baking soda, baking powder, butter, salt, and buttermilk to the mix until it is well blended.**
- **Step three: Prep waffle iron**

It didn't take me until I got to step three to realize that this wasn't going to happen. I thought, *Great, that's a lot of stuff…even with this extra time, I'll still be late for school. I don't know how Mom can do this every day.* I closed the cookbook in front of me.

Mission aborted.

Since preparing breakfast was out of the question this morning, I decided to just relax and watch the news until it was time to go. Nothing was really on except the usual: weather and traffic. Sometime over the course of watching I must have fallen asleep because the next thing I knew, my two brothers were downstairs eating and my mom was saluting us with a piece of toast as she walked out the door.

Hmmm, she must have woken me up.

I made my way from the couch to the pitcher of orange juice sitting on the counter. My two brothers paid me no mind as they continued stuffing their faces. I leaned my back against the counter and sipped my drink slowly.

"Good morning."

Jason turned back at me and said the same. He was just about done eating, so he had made his way over to the newspaper. Watching Jay work was like watching a work of art or a piece of finely crafted machinery. He scanned the articles robotically, stopping only to nitpick over the most essential details. "It's going to start to get even colder next week," he said.

"I know. I watched the news this morning," I said.

"OK."

And that was that.

Jason and I really didn't get along too much when we were growing up. Even now he's considered the brash one of the pack. We would always bump heads on every single issue, given the opportunity. It wasn't like we wanted to argue; it just happened. I think it had to do with the fact that we were polar opposites. As kids we were always at war. If it wasn't one thing it was another. My first missing tooth was from him. My first broken bone was from him too, as was my first black eye and many other things.

If I had to categorize him as anything, I would say that he's more a rival than an enemy. He's always been a driving force in my life…whether he realizes it or not. Part of that was how I was always being compared to him.

CHAPTER 3

WITH THE SMART KIDS; A FLASHBACK

JASON AND I BOTH WENT to the same middle school. He was and still is a genius, nothing short of brilliant. On the other hand, I wasn't as gifted. I mean I wasn't bad, but I wasn't a "Jason" either. When he graduated from middle school, he was immediately accepted to a prestigious high school in the city. Everyone was proud of him, of course, but the pressures to follow in my brother's footsteps were instantly placed on me. In the upcoming years, my parents would try to place me into G. T. (gifted and talented) classes and higher-learning programs over the summer. As I got closer to graduation from middle school, the number one question was, "What high school are you going to attend?" Then they would follow up with, "You're going to be a Tom Cat like your brother, right?"

"Sure." That's all I could come up with for a response. "I'd like to, but if I don't get in, it won't bother me." But truthfully it would and it did.

During the remainder of my middle-school years, I felt a constant tug on my heart to upstage Jason. It was actually a mix of emotions and, to this day, I still really can't describe how I felt. I wanted my parents to understand me as an individual, but at the same time, I wanted to show them I could do it—especially Jason. While this whole thing was playing out, Jason would always find ways to push my buttons. When I would get my tests back, he would glance over them and whisper little remarks from over my parent's shoulders. "Really, a C? Is that the best he can do?"

He wasn't shy about it either. Sometimes he made sure I could hear him; other times he said them directly to my face. I remember one time I came home with an F from a math test I had studied relentlessly for. He must have overheard my parents talking about it, because when he asked me about it later, I told him I did OK but not as good as I had hoped. In response he just looked at me with a smirk and said, "Oh, so I guess you really are the stupid one of the family." I was devastated…but it was true. In comparison to him, I was stupid. He had achieved so many things while I, on the other hand, had nothing to vouch for. Looking back at his transcripts, he had virtually all A's, and I couldn't even manage a GPA of 2.8.

For my eighth-grade year, I had a checklist of things I wanted to do before I graduated. I wanted to kiss a girl, ask out my crush, but most importantly, I wanted to get at least a 3.0 for the year; none of them actually happened, though.

I remember the day before graduation, when we all got our grades back. I was hesitant to open my envelope. All my other classmates ripped through them, eager to see how they stood at the end of the year, comparing themselves to one another to see who came out on top. It even got to the point where they would badger the shyer kids to open their envelopes or else they would do it themselves. In the past they would ask me what I got and I would simply respond, "A 2.9, only one point away from a 3.0." Usually that was enough to convince them and get them off my back, but since this was the very last report card unveiling, only physical evidence would suffice.

One of the kids came up to me and asked, "Hey, what did you finish with? I got a 3.2."

"I don't know," I said, but, in fact, I did know. The night before I had calculated my grades, and it came out to a 2.6. After all of my hard work, all I could manage was a 2.6.

"Well, open it and find out."

"No," I said, "my parents don't let me. I'll get in trouble if they see the seal is broken."

That was the only excuse I could come up with.

"Come on, Alex, just open it! I'm sure they won't mind."

Before he was even finished with his sentence, his arm came lashing toward my envelope. He clasped it, but just before he had a tight grip on it, I quickly jerked it away and smiled. "Rules are rules."

He withdrew his hand. "Whatever," he said and walked away. That was a close one.

When I got home later that day, my parents were also eager to see what was in that oh-so-magical envelope. Usually they would just beat around the bush, but that day they went straight to business. The whole family was eating dinner that night when the topic arose. My dad raised his head from his meal. "I heard you got your report card in."

"Yeah"

"OK, let me see it." My body stiffened and a feverish chill slid down my spine.

"OK, here," I said. I had already come prepared. I knew this was going to happen sooner or later so I brought it with me to the dinner table just in case. I took my time getting the envelope from inside my book sack beside me. As I raised my head up from beneath the dinner table, it felt like all eyes were on me. The tension grew thicker as I placed the tan envelope on the edge of the table. Suddenly the room became quiet. I slowly eased the letter across the table for what seemed like miles, until it finally tipped my dad's hand. He picked it up and waved it at me. "I'll be sure to read this later," he said, and we then continued eating dinner.

I had dodged a bullet that night at the dinner table. He too wanted me to get at least a 3.0 for my final run, and if he had seen my report card that night, disappointment would have been all over his face. Lucky for me he didn't see it till after graduation.

The big day had finally come. I was dressed head to toe in my Sunday best, waiting in line along with my other classmates. We were thrilled, but at the same time, we had mixed emotions. I could hear my classmates saying their farewells, while others were crying in the background. We were happy that we were about to start a new chapter in our lives, but at the same time, we were sad to see that this one was coming to a close. Over the course of the years that we had been part of the school, we had formed strong ties with both the staff and each other. On these grounds we had forged lifelong relationships and bonds that would never be broken. I guess this was such an emotional moment because we finally realized just how much history we had here.

The chapel grew quiet. One of the teachers peered out from behind the doors and signaled at us to calm down. She turned back and whispered, "The ceremony is about to start." As she closed the door, she put emphasis on the finger over her lip, asking us again to settle down. From the other side of the door, I could hear the principal's muffled voice. "Tonight we are gathered here to congratulate your children, the class of 2004. Over the years we have seen them grow and walk though the many chapters in life. Tonight they stand before you as they end this one and boldly enter another."

As he spoke a knot began to grow in my stomach. I hadn't noticed it before, but the tension was really starting to mount. My shoulders began to tense up, and sweat began to accumulate on my palms. Thoughts began to swirl all around my head. Will I trip? What if they don't call my name? Where's the person who's supposed to be in front of me? Fear had gripped me and dragged me into the darkness. I was engulfed by my doubt and paralyzed by my emotions. My muscles tensed, and my body began to react to the coldness around me. As the speech went on, I felt like I was slipping further and further away.

Just when I thought all hope was lost, a hand stretched forth and brought me back into the light. The teacher snapped and quickly directed our attention to her. "Now class, remember what we went over in rehearsal." *That's right.* We'd practiced this weeks in advance. "The ceremony will be getting underway shortly. Pat yourselves on the back; you've all done a great job." As she continued to speak, I felt fear's grip on my body slowly releasing. I thought, *She's right. We've practiced this countless times. We got this.*

Our teacher pressed her ear closer to the door, as she waited for the signal to begin the march. "And now, ladies and gentlemen, I present to you the class of 2004!" She leaped back and motioned us to go, opening the doors in front of her. As they opened, lights were flashing and a sea of people was in our midst. We continued our march single file to the front rows of the chapel and sat down.

From this point on, things really got blurry. The adrenaline was really pumping, so everything seemed to be moving fast. After we sat down, the principal began another speech, and before I knew it, we were at the awards part of the ceremony. Perfect attendance, outstanding conduct, no tardy slips, and other minute rewards were handed out first. But things really got interesting when they started to commend the students who had achieved the honor roll.

I, as well as some of my other classmates waited patiently in the pews. Some waited for their names to be called and others for it to be over with. This part of the ceremony was the worst part to me; instead of acknowledging who did well, it always seemed to have a way of pointing out the ones that had missed the mark. I can only speak for myself, because that's the way it always happened to me, especially since I was known as the kid who never revealed his report card. Ironically, for some reason, when my classmates tried to put a finger on me, they always described me as the smart kid. Tonight they were going to be sadly disabused. I had only managed to get a 2.6 during the last quarter, and when my name wasn't called out, everyone would know the truth. Finally the mystery of Alex's grades would come to a close, leaving only disappointment in its wake. My parents still hadn't seen my report card, and I knew deep down they wanted to see me walk proudly onto that stage with the other kids, the smart kids.

As I sat in my seat, my own thoughts numbed me to what was going on. With every name the principal shouted out, the closer he moved to where my name would be.

"Annette Fisher."

The tension started to build. Little by little he started to make his way to the Rs.

"Susan Little"

For every name called, it felt like a weight was bearing down on my shoulders.

"John Marquette."

"Joshua Mason."

"Pauline Nader."

I thought, *Great, he's making his way to the Os. He's almost there.* I sank in my seat. It was too much for me. My palms grew even sweatier as I gripped my pant leg. With every name he called, it felt like he was chipping away at my soul.

"Cory Orlando."

"Jordan Patrick."

"Terica Patrick."

It wasn't so much that I didn't make the honor roll that bothered me but more so the disappointment I felt was because others would know. It's a horrible feeling to know you let someone down. Without even looking back, I could tell that they were all waiting in pure anticipation. I could feel their eyes clawing down my back, and with every name called, their nails ran deeper and deeper.

"Julia Patterson."

That one ran deep. But I could still feel them raving for more.

"Ryan Peterson."

My eyes widened. The Ps were done and we were now on the Rs.

"Jacob Roberson."

"Zack Robertson."

I closed my eyes and winced as pain ran down my spine; my stomach began to flip.

"Alex Rogers."

When I heard my name, I opened my eyes and looked toward the principal. My body went numb.

"Alex Rogers."

He called it again. This time I was sure that it wasn't a mistake. I tried to move, but my body was frozen stiff. From the corner of the chapel, I heard something that began to melt the ice around me. Behind me I could hear the cheers of my family egging me on to claim my reward. I stood up and made my way toward the stage. With every step I took, I could hear my family getting louder and louder. With every step I took, I could feel them behind me, pushing me forward. It actually felt like my family was walking with me. For the first time in a long time, I felt that they were proud of me. Maybe all along they were aching for a moment to be proud of me, but until then I had never really given them anything to be proud about.

When I was in arm's reach, the principal said, "Good job," pulled me close, and hugged me. He then directed me to go stand with the other kids. As I walked across the stage, I scanned the audience. A stream of applause came pouring down when I finally took my place among the other students. I turned and faced the crowd.

The principal continued calling out names, while I looked over the chapel. Suddenly he stopped. "Before you stand the students who have made the honor roll." And with that came the ovation. Cheers flooded the room, and a second wave of clapping rushed in. As I looked out into the crowd, I spotted my parents and stared my mother straight in the eyes and thought, *Look at me now. I'm finally up here. I'm finally here with the smart kids.* As I thought it, a tear rolled down the side of my cheek. I know this isn't possible, and it may sound crazy, but mom must have heard my thoughts that day, because after I thought it, she starting crying too. I liked to think that she realized at that moment that I had made it. She was crying because her son had finally made it with the smart kids.

After the ceremony ended, I decided to wait on the steps of the chapel for the crowd to clear out. I really didn't think about it when it was happening, but after everything was over, I wondered how I had got called up in the first place. I knew I had a 2.6, yet I got an award for having at least a 3.0. As I sat on the steps, I started to review all of the possible explanations, but none really fit the bill. Maybe they felt sorry for me and just gave it to me anyway. Maybe I didn't calculate my grade right in the first place. Maybe it was a miracle, who knows? I just figured that I should at least enjoy the moment while it was here. I'd think about the rest tomorrow.

A few more moments passed, and more people poured out of the chapel; I watched them as they trickled down the steps. As I sat there watching them go, I realized that life was perfect. I looked up to the sky and let out a sigh of relief.

It was nighttime now. The sky was beautiful. The stars were actually out tonight, which was rare for the city. As I waited I wondered what was taking my family so long to come out. Not that it mattered. I wouldn't know what to say when they found me. Should I even say anything? What was there to say? Nothing but congratulations and a pat on the back, I guess.

I propped my arms back to support myself against the steps. *When are they going to get here?* I wondered. Sitting there it was hard to censor my thoughts. So many things were running across my mind. The rush was causing the ideas to flow. In an attempt to level out, I flicked my head up at the stars again and watched them twinkle in the moonlight.

You know…when you look at the stars individually, they seem to move to their own beat. But if you take a step back and look at the big picture, all of the other ones seem to be moving along with it. It's kind of like life… if each individual star is like a moment in life, it makes perfect sense. You can only live your life one moment at a time. Sometimes you feel like you're not going anywhere or doing anything, and you wonder how it'll all turn out, but suddenly you make it to your destination one day, and all you can do is look back and wonder how you got there. It may not make sense at first glance, but that's the way I see it; life's a constellation. The individual moments in our lives seem so pointless sometimes; but when you look at the whole picture, you can see that those little moments have formed memories.

As I gazed up at the stars, I began to count them out There were way too many. I dropped my head down and began to stare at my feet until a tap on my shoulder interrupted me. It was my mom and the rest of my family. I stood up and greeted them with a hug, and we began to walk toward the car. For the rest of the night, I was bombarded with a series of questions. During the whole ride home, my dad kept on asking me why I didn't tell them. I just smiled; I couldn't have told him anything because I myself had no idea until it happened.

As I rode in the backseat, I peered out of the window and watched the traffic move by. Soon enough my mind began to flow with it. Thoughts began to stream about in my head. I couldn't help but question how I had made it. Eventually when they opened my report card, they would figure it out anyway. The more I thought about it, the more it dampened my mood. Now that I thought about it, it was like I was pretty much living out a lie…How long did I want to keep this up? The longer this went on, the harder it would be to tell them the truth. "Hey, where do you want to go to celebrate?" My mom turned to me from the passenger side.

"Where do you want to go?...Alex?"

I turned from the window. "Hmmm? Oh…I'm OK; we can just head home."

"You sure? It's only right that we celebrate today. You earned it, baby."

"No, it's OK, Mom. I just want to go home…it's been a long day."

"Whatever you say, champ."

It's funny. Out of all the words in the English dictionary, her word choice had to include "earned." That pretty much put the nail in the coffin. It went pretty deep too. I cringed to myself a little bit. I hadn't earned anything.

I didn't get the honor roll, but still, they decided to call me up there anyway. I appreciated their act of kindness, but it wasn't right. I didn't deserve to be standing up there with the others; I didn't deserve that honor. It...*hurt*...but, truthfully, what hurt the most was that I would have to be the bearer of bad news. I could deal with not making the honor roll, but living this lie was killing me inside. They let me up there out of sympathy. I didn't deserve to be up there with the rest of them. It was my last quarter, and they knew I tried hard so they decided to call my name anyway. An honorable mention of some sort; nothing more nothing less.

The ride home was short lived; we were home before we knew it—not enough time to prepare. Sadly, that's usually how most things in life tend to end up. Sometimes you get blindsided by something you never see coming; it hits home, and more often than not, the results are devastating. Time is always an issue, and sometimes we simply just don't have enough of it. The way I learned that lesson was through the help of an old friend.

Growing up I met this girl who was one of my friend's cousins. She seemed to be perfectly normal on the outside. Beautiful in every which way, shape, or form; but one day at his house, she was acting a little strange, and eventually she ended up rushing to the bathroom. I was a little confused and asked him what was wrong. He told me that she was just recently diagnosed with stage-two lung cancer, and she was just getting used to the chemo. A few moments later, she returned and everything was fine. I thought so anyway.

As the months went by, I began to notice her condition was getting worse and worse, but still, every time I asked her if she was OK, she always said, "I'm fine." Even in her later stages, she never really told me what was wrong, probably because she really didn't want me to see her differently. From the time that I first met her till she was on her death bed, she always seemed to put up a strong front, even with the simplest things, like when we played hide and seek. When she was healthier, she would always find ways to be the seeker. She even tricked me into believing that because she was older she got to make up the rules. She would always find me relatively easily. The fun part would be finding her. She was so good that she let me count to fifteen before I could look for her. Even with that, she was still almost impossible to find. But that was then…

As her condition worsened, it became easier and easier to find her. As time went by, I noticed I would have to count slower or add numbers to the count. She was getting slower. When I called out for her to tell her that I was coming, she would come out from hiding and say, "Alex, I need more time." At her prime the count was up to fifteen, but by our last game, it was at ninety. It got to the point where she only walked to her hiding spot, because it was too much stress on her lungs to jog, and even if she did make it to a hiding place in time, she would eventually begin to cough and give her position away. She wouldn't act like it was a big deal. She'd just emerge from hiding and say, "Let's go home…we played enough today."

I remember one day in particular when we were playing. The last time we played. It was about seven months after she was diagnosed. I placed my head on the tree and began to count. In my head I knew it wasn't too safe to be playing. It was cold outside, and it wasn't good for Jessie's lungs. But she said she was OK, she'd be fine. I thought as I continued the count. "No peeking! You're getting too good at this. I figure since I quit my job I would have time to get better at this, but you're a pro, Al! Remember, count to ninety!" I smiled and kept counting as I heard her footsteps shrink away in the distance. She was running. "Ready or not, here I come!" I shouted as I began to search. It didn't take me too long to find her. She had her back turned away from a house in the neighborhood, so I snuck up on her. As I inched closer, I noticed that she was resting her head on one of her arms with the other over her mouth. She must have heard me, because when I was within arm's reach, she turned around and looked at me straight in the eyes. At that moment my attention was fixated on her blue eyes. She was crying.

"Why are you crying?"

Tears welled up in her eyes and she shook her head.

"What's wrong?"

She started to shake her head as the tears flowed. But still, not a word from her.

"Jessie…"

I stood in shock and stared at her, as she cried. That's all I could do. She let out a sob and blood began to trickle down from her hand covering her mouth. She coughed and more blood leaked through her clasped hand. She saw that I was scared, so she came toward me and hugged me. She hugged me for what seemed like forever. Time had stopped, but even so all she could say as she held me was "Alex…I need more time." I gripped her tighter and began to cry as well. It didn't take her long to regain her composure though. She was strong. She wiped her nose and held my hand as she walked me back to my house. Not much was said. It wasn't like anything else could have been said. Out of all the things she could have in the world, all she wanted was more time, but no one could give it to her.

That winter Jessie passed away. She was only seventeen. I wasn't there when she passed though. As things got worse, my mom forbade me to visit. She said I shouldn't put myself through such torture. I guess she was right. It was painful to watch Jessie deteriorate in front of me. But I had to do it. I finally found a way to repay her. She had given so much of her time to me. Even through the later stages of her sickness, she was always there for me, so I figured I would repay the favor. I couldn't give her more time on Earth, but while she was here, I thought I could at least give her the next best thing: more time on Earth with me.

If she had been alive at my graduation, she would have only been nineteen, and if she were alive now, she would be in her twenties. I used to tell her all the time that when I graduated I wanted her to sit on the front row and clap for me. But if she knew what was going on now, she wouldn't have approved. I banged my head against the glass softly, and then stepped out of the car. *Ugh. Jessie…what was the point in taking her life away?*

I called out in the distance as I shut the door. "Hey Mom…I'm going for a walk, OK?" She nodded. I turned my back to her and began my trek. I wasn't more than halfway down the block when she called out my name.

"Alex. Something wrong?"

I stopped in my tracks and turned around. I didn't want to lie to her, so I just clenched my fist in my pockets. I wanted to tell her that everything was wrong. Nothing was right about this night.

"You can come if you like…I'm just going around the block."

"OK…Sounds like a plan to me."

"Well, hurry and catch up."

I turned back around and started walking slowly. She picked up the pace until she was trailing a little behind me. It didn't take long for her to start probing me.

"How ya feeling?"

I turned my head and looked toward her. She had a genuine look on her face. I turned my head back and continued to watch my feet as they pushed off the pavement.

"Fine…It's just a little too much, ya know? It kinda just hit me…I'm still absorbing it all."

The whole time I was talking, she looked at me, but I couldn't look back. How long could I keep this up? It felt like every step I took was leading me further and further away from the truth. I really wanted to say something, but my mouth wouldn't move. I couldn't say anything, so I continued to walk as far as I possibly could. I just wanted to get away from my problems. I knew it didn't make any sense, but that was what was in my head. Maybe if I just kept on walking, one day it wouldn't matter anymore, then I could just go home. It was wishful thinking, but I really didn't want to put up with living a lie every day for the rest of my life. I was lost.

I must have picked up the pace without even knowing, because when I glanced to the right of me, no one was there. I checked my other side; she wasn't there either. I turned around, and she was trailing behind me again. I slowed down but still kept my stride. I heard her call from behind me.

"What's wrong, baby? You don't have to lie to me… tell me."

She placed her hand on my shoulder from behind, and I stopped as she turned me toward her. She put her hands on both sides of my face.

"Tell me what's wrong, baby. It hurts to see you like this. Don't try to hide it. I've raised you, so I know when something's bothering you…just tell me."

I was still looking at the ground, even though my face was in her hands. If I looked up now, tears would follow.

"What's wrong?"

"What if your best isn't enough, Mom…? I mean like, what if you try, try, and try again, and it still isn't enough? What do you do then? What do you do when no matter what you try to do—and you try really hard, the hardest you've ever tried for something in your entire life—but you still fall short? What do you do?"

The tears began to flow. She wiped my cheeks with her thumbs.

"Alex"

"What options do you have left, when you're just not good enough, Mom? I just want to be good enough. I didn't make it into the same school as Jason because I wasn't good enough. I didn't make the honor roll all these years because I wasn't good enough, and even now, when I really tried my hardest, as hard as I could, it still wasn't good enough to get the honor roll. What's wrong with me?"

I sank my head into my mother's chest.

"Every time we had to take a test, they would ask me what my grades were, but I would have to lie because they just weren't good enough. It isn't fair, Mom. I would pay attention in class and study during recess, while all they did was joke around. Even at home I would study all night—you saw me. But still, they would pass while I failed. It doesn't even make sense, Mom. How come they were better than me?"

I paused to wipe the tears on my cheek with her shirt.

"Even when I wasn't at school, everyone would still compare me to Jason. You, Dad, everyone...you guys put me in the same middle school as him; you guys want me to go to the same high school as him, and probably the same college as him, at this rate. Correct me if I'm wrong, but I've noticed something. I'm nowhere near as smart as he is, so just give up on me. I'll never live up to the Jason you all want me to be, so you can stop it already. You'll only be disappointed in the end. I'm just not good enough, so let me be."

I leaned in closer and clutched my mom as she began to stroke the top of my head.

"Listen, Alex, sometimes in life, you can try as hard as you can, but simply it's still not enough, but that doesn't mean that you were stupid or you weren't good enough; you tried your best and, in the end, that's all you can do. It's not your fault if it was the best you could do...if you can look back and say that you've honestly given it your all, that you've done all you can, you should have no regrets. Just put it behind you and move forward. And if you weren't pleased with your results, remember what you did wrong and learn from them, so you'll be ready next time. And if you feel your best isn't good enough, try, try, and try, again, so that one day, when you look at all of your accomplishments, you'll realize that you've come a long way. That's all I ask, Alex. I just want you to try your best.

"Sometimes in life, you can try as hard as you can, but things simply don't come out as well as they should. It doesn't mean it's your fault. It's just the way things ended up…if you think you're stupid, you're mistaken. None of my babies are stupid. You've tried your best…and that's all I ask. I know you're upset about not making the honor roll…and, to be honest, we already knew about it. Your father and I went over it last night. It was nice of them to call you up there even though you didn't make it, but in all honestly it didn't even matter. Up there or not, we still would have been proud of you; you're our son. No matter what you do, we'll always be proud of you. I'm so sorry that we put so much pressure on you. I had no idea that you felt this way. I'm so sorry I put you through that.

She pulled me in closer. I could feel her tears falling on the top of my head.

"I never meant to put you through that. We were so caught up in raising you like Jason we forgot that you're your own person. You have your own likes and dislikes, your own fears, your own ambitions, your own dreams, your own life…but somewhere along the line, we forgot that. You're your own person, Alex, and you're beautiful. I don't want you to ever forget that."

After she said that, we just stood there and hugged. That night it felt like I got a lot off my chest that had been plaguing me for a while. I even got closer to my mother through it. Before we went back in the house, she stopped and said something to me in the doorway.

"Alex, you know I love you, no matter what you do, right? It doesn't matter what your grades are or anything like that…I'll always love you."

"Yeah, Mom, I know."

She rubbed my head as we stepped through the door.

Later that week we got the results from the admissions test. Unfortunately I didn't get in, but I was OK with that. I knew that I did the best that I could, and that was all I had to offer. I gave it my all, and that was all I could do; so looking back at it, I had no regrets. Now, all that was left was for me to move forward.

∽

I took another sip of my orange juice as I shifted focus back to the present. The juice was still too pulpy, so I swirled my glass a little and took another sip. It just wasn't that good this morning. Jason folded the paper and stood up.

"How long are you going to be standing over there, Al?"

He nudged me over as he approached the pitcher.

"I just woke up…I'm still a little zoned out. Been thinking, ya know."

I poured the juice out into the sink beside me.

"You know it's bad, right? It doesn't taste too good to me."

He took a sip from his glass and placed it on the table and walked out the door.

"Tastes fine to me…maybe it's just you."

The door shut behind him.

Maybe…

I got my books ready for school and left the house shortly after Jay. Even though it had been only a couple of days, it seemed like I hadn't been to school in forever. It was cold today, almost too cold. The frost ground at my face as I walked down the road.

It should be getting warm soon, I thought. My hands were still freezing even though I had gloves on. Even stuffing them in my pockets was no use. My breath etched ghostly silhouettes into the atmosphere as I exhaled. On some of the cars that passed me, I could see frost plastered on the windows. It didn't really matter to them, though. They were warm in there...so lucky; moments like these reminded me of the good ol' days when my mom would drop me off at school. I was really lucky to have that back then...especially in times like these. I guess you don't know what you've got until it's gone.

When I got to school, it was the same old same old. Students were few and far between in the early mornings, except for the usual crew. I walked down the hall toward my locker to change out my books for the day.

Fourteen...twenty-four...thirty-six...

Voila. It opened. I really hated locks to be honest; I could never remember if it was left right left, or right left right, plus my luck with them wasn't too great to begin with.

OK, I need my chemistry, english, history, and algebra books...I think I have homework in algebra due today. I grabbed my notebook and shuffled through the pages. *OK, Friday's notes...*

I skimmed through the pages, looking between the scribbles and doodles that gave evidence of where my attention had been that evening. Ugh. "Section Review Chapters 2-4. Even numbers." *Figures...just my luck.* If I rushed it, I might finish in time to make it to my first class. I slammed my locker shut and began to peruse my notebook as I rushed toward the library. I shouldn't be so careless...no way I was going to finish all this work, let alone get it all right in time. I picked up the pace. My head was buried in my notes, looking over what we had gone through that Friday. I didn't bother to look up. I relied on my instincts to drive me to my destination. Usually they tended to point me in the right direction, but today seemed to be the exception. Out of all the things that could have gone wrong, I had to cross paths with Rasheed.

While I was walking, I bumped into him—well, more or less; he bumped into me. To be honest, I had forgotten about him during my hiatus from school. It seemed that now was the time to face reality.

My path had run its course, and the obstacle was set before me, a five-foot, ten-inch, one hundred sixty-five-pound roadblock to be exact. If I wanted to finish my work, I had to get out of this situation as quickly as possible.

"'Sup, faggot?"

I sidestepped and tried to walk to the left. At first he stood and watched in amazement, but he quickly snapped to his senses and cut me off again.

"Hey…I'm talking to you."

From his voice I could tell he was agitated. But I couldn't just stand there and entertain this. I really didn't understand people sometimes; he really looked forward to this. How could he find pleasure by making my life worse? He just saw me, so he instantly changed his top priority to make my life miserable…it was starting to get on my nerves. I attempted to sidestep him again, but he blocked my escape route once more.

"What's the rush, fag boy?"

"If you're talking to me, I only respond to Alex…but judging from how eager you are to talk to me, you seem like the fag…And I'm not really in a rush; it's just that I don't swing that way, that's all."

The tension in the air suddenly became dense. The smirk on his face quickly turned into a snarl. I think I hit a nerve. He took a step closer, leaving us face to face. He directed his attention solely to me, tuning away from the outside world as he glared into my eyes. I really needed to go to the library. This was ridiculous. He'd started all this, and now he got mad when someone stood up to him. *This morning sucks.*

"Look, Rasheed. I have something important I need to handle before the bell rings…I have to go."

His face cringed as he grit he teeth. He clinched his fist, and his eyes widened. *He's about to swing at me,* I thought. I stepped back a little.

"Let me go…I really need to get this work d—"

"I don't care about what you have to do." He cut me off.

He slapped my books out of my hand. All I could do was watch my notes flutter to the ground, scattering across the hallway floor as they landed individually.

"Now, pick them up."

I actually thought about picking them up…but I had to stop myself from kneeling down on the ground. He probably would have kicked me in the face, so I stared him down.

"Pick 'em up."

I could sense the agitation in his voice, but I didn't budge, I just kept looking him dead in his eyes.

"I said pick them up."

He pushed me.

"I'm not gonna ask you again…pick them up."

I just kept on looking at him. The last thing I needed was to be called to the principal's office. I just needed him to get bored with this and walk away. All I wanted to do was get the work done, and if I got into trouble, I'd be in the office at least till homeroom was over.

He grabbed my shirt and shoved me against the lockers. I looked to the left and saw the clock posted in the hallway above the doors.

Seven forty-five…fifteen minutes left, I thought.

He cocked his fist back and set his sights dead on my face. Now he was making a scene.

"All I want to do is go to the library and finish my math homework…all this isn't necessary…just let me go."

He paused for a second. It seemed to me that he actually took the time to think reasonably. He took his weight off me and lowered his fist. He loosened his grip, and his expression turned to normal. I was skeptical until he stepped away from me and began to pick up my papers. After some thought I came around and began to help him, in the process ignoring my instincts.

"Thanks."

"For what?"

That same cocky smirk that he had earlier slowly began to emerge from the corners of his mouth. He turned the papers that he had amassed horizontally in his hand and looked into my eyes as he began to rip them apart, piece by piece. With each and every tear, I felt more and more of my consciousness slip into frustration and rage. He even laughed as he tore the final piece and tossed it on the ground as he rose up.

"Next time I tell you to do something, do it. *Now,* pick it up…"

I actually believed him…I should have known it was too good to be true. I had actually believed he would have reasoned with me just like that. No ifs, ands, or buts about it. No one is that complacent. Now I'd lost half my notes as a punishment for being so naïve…and on top of that

I couldn't even complete the assignment. This made no sense. Why would he do this to me? Did he want me to kill him? Didn't he realize that you couldn't just mess around people's lives like this? I got up and stared at him laughing at me…he actually thought this was funny. I shoved him and I screamed the thoughts coming to my mind.

"You think it's funny? All I was trying to do was finish my work, and you just decide that it's OK to just do what you see fit and trash my notes? Are you retarded? Do you just wake up every morning and wonder whose life you can make worse for the day?"

I kept on shoving him.

"You think you're all high and mighty, but all you do is work off of fear. I'm not even afraid of you. You're a waste of sperm. You were probably a mistake. Your mom probably doesn't even love you. How could she? You're failing every subject, and all you do at school is get in trouble. Is that why you do all of this? How about you man up and do something with your life, because at the end of the day you're still a failure if this is your life's work."

He was against a locker of his own now. I must have snapped because I didn't realize that any of this was happening. Well, I kind of did, but it was like I was running on autopilot and couldn't take over. Rasheed was taken aback too. The roles were reversed. He was the one with his back against the wall. I drew back my fist and took aim at his face. I had a million and one reasons to hit him, but this recent one was more than enough to suffice for the damage he'd done. Rasheed was still shocked, and I had my opportunity, but I couldn't bring myself to closure. Every fiber of my being wanted to do it, but I couldn't pull the trigger.

"Is there a problem, gentlemen?" A voice from behind us broke the tension.

I looked over my shoulder to place a name to the voice. It was the principal, Mr. Turner. I lowered my fist and backed away from Rasheed. Mr. Turner further separated us. I didn't think he quite understood what was going on.

"I think we have matters to discuss in my office."

He signaled for us to walk alongside him, Rasheed at the right and me on the left. I bet he was confused right about now. This whole scene was backward; I was the perceived aggressor and Rasheed was at my mercy. Key word *perceived*. If he had come five seconds later, what would have happened? Would I have hit him? I didn't think so…I think.

By now everyone was staring at what had happened earlier. Mr. Turner tried his best to avert the attention elsewhere, but it was to no avail. As we walked down the hall, my eyes drifted toward the tiles. Several of my classmates stopped in their tracks to see what was going on. I avoided eye contact. I didn't want to be bothered. Over and over in my head, I went over the course of events, wondering how it had gone this far. It could have been numerous things…I should have just walked away. It was all because I almost hit him. That's why I was in this predicament.

Looking down at my unclenched fist, I realized exactly what I had gotten myself into. I had every reason to hit him, but I couldn't do it; but I should have…that was just one more thing that made us different.

We arrived at the door of the office shortly after the bell rang. Mr. Turner walked in ahead of us while we waited outside.

"Ms. Bridget, forward all of my calls to the front desk. I have business to attend to with these two." He pointed at us through the see-through window. Ms. Bridget peeped her head out from behind the desk and motioned us to come in.

"Take a seat gentlemen; the principal will see you shortly."

I walked in first, with Rasheed behind me. From the look of it, he seemed like he was at home. I was nervous though. It was my first time being called to the principal's office. I was reluctant to take my seat. I knew that once I sat down I wouldn't be able to leave until the whole thing was over with. As I sat down, Mr. Turner walked into his office, shutting the door behind him. All I could do now was wait. I glanced over at Rasheed, but he paid me no mind. He was probably getting his story together. I should have been doing the same…even though there wasn't much to say.

I was trying to get my work done and he wouldn't leave me alone…so I was about to hit him and…then you showed up.

No, that wouldn't work…

I went to my locker this morning, as usual, to switch out my books. I had an assignment due for first block, so I rushed over to the library. On the way I bumped into Rasheed, and that's how the whole thing started. He was harassing me, and I just wanted to do my work. I tried to tell him I was busy, but he still wouldn't leave me alone. He hit the books out of my hand and then pretended like he would help me pick them up…and then he ripped them up. I guess that's when I snapped.

No…too little detail. I needed to get this right. Who knew what Rasheed would say?

This morning I went to my locker to get my books. I had a math assignment that I forgot to do last night, so I was rushing to the library to get it done. On my way I bumped into Rasheed and that's how the whole thing started. I tried to tell him that I had things to do, but he didn't want to hear it. I tried to avoid the situation, but he kept on harassing me. When he knocked my books to the ground and tore up my notes…well, that was the last straw. This whole school year he's been giving me nothing but trouble. I just couldn't take it anymore. That's why when you saw me; things looked the way they did…for once I actually tried to stick up for myself. Sure, if he told me something I told him something back, but actions speak louder than words. So I decided to take action. Words don't seem to work with him.

Ugh. Still not perfect but it was a good start. I looked over at Rasheed again. He returned fire with an angry stare. He didn't want to be in this situation either, but he'd brought this on himself. I hoped he realized it. In the corner of my eye I saw Mr. Turner's head pop out from behind his office door.

"Rasheed."

I thought we were both going to be in the room at the same time, but instead he separated us and decided to let us tell our own story individually. I should have seen this coming. Rasheed slowly got up from his chair, refusing to break eye contact with me until it was absolutely necessary. Within seconds he was gone. I watched him until the door closed behind him. He was on trial now and Mr. Turner was the ultimate judge. In this school he held life and death in his hands. Hopefully when my judgment came, I'd be prepared. I folded my arms and stared at the door, waiting for my time to come. I began to recite my story over and over in my head, making sure I had even the littlest details correct. I tried to focus on my story—the truth, but I began to wonder what Rasheed was telling him. I kept on telling myself it didn't matter…all that mattered was my side of the story. I just had to present it in a way that he knew was real.

It must have been at least thirty minutes before the door opened up again. Rasheed left the room with the same expression he had when he came in. Now it was my turn. I heard Mr. Turner call me from his office. I got up and walked into the room and closed the door behind me.

"Take a seat."

I grabbed the seat in front me and anchored my way down into the chair. At the same time, he walked behind his desk and sat down. He reached for the manila folder on his desk. It had my name on it.

"Alex Rogers," he said with a monotone voice as he scanned the inside of the folder.

"You really don't seem to be a trouble maker…rarely missed school, good GPA, no behavioral problems…how did you end up in here exactly?" He smiled and waited for my reply.

I was taken back. I couldn't answer, so he continued to speak.

"Rasheed I can understand, but you not so much….So far I've only heard Rasheed's side of the story, and I can't pass judgment until I hear yours as well." He scanned through my folder again.

"So what exactly happened, Alex?" He lowered the folder from his face and stared directly at me with an eager smile stretching across the length of his face.

"Well…"

I began to speak. Mr. Turner leaned forward in his chair and propped his elbows on the desk, interlacing his hands as he waited attentively for me to state my piece. I was still a little nervous, but I knew my final judgment depended on what I said. Court was now in session.

"Well…in the past, Rasheed's been giving me trouble, so this is nothing new. We had our little run-ins but today was different. Today I had an assignment that was due fairly early in the day. I only found out about it this morning when I went to go change my books…so you see, I was rushing to get that work done."

I paused for a second and took a deep breath. Here was where it would count.

"That's when it all happened. On my way to the library, I ran into Rasheed. I tried to avoid him, but he wouldn't let me be. He picked the fight with me. I thought at first it would be another pointless exchange of words, but eventually it got to the point where he tore my notes in half. Soon after that was when you walked in on us…while he was ripping my notes; that's why I snapped. All this time he's been bullying me around for no reason; today just happened to be the day I took a stand for myself. What you saw was me just taking that stand. I didn't hit him, but I do admit I caused a scene. At least now I bet he won't be messing with me."

As I said the last part, the principal's facial expression changed. He grinned and rose from his seat.

I stopped talking.

"I don't mean to be rude, but are you done?" He pushed his chair back from underneath the desk. I nodded.

"Yes, sir."

"OK, well I'm going to call Rasheed in so we can settle things."

He walked past me and peeped his head out of the door.

"Ms. Bridget, can you please send Rasheed in again?"

After he shut the door, I heard her muffled voice direct Rasheed to come back. When he entered the room, he looked the same as before: unnerved. I wondered what he and Mr. Turner had talked about when it was just them. He sat down in the chair beside me. Mr. Turner made himself at home as well. He sat down with his body in the same position as before. It felt like I was on trial again.

"So, after hearing both sides of the story, I don't have much to say."

He looked over at Rasheed.

"Rasheed, it is clear to me that you were the instigator of this whole propaganda. While your story contradicts Alex's, it seems unbelievable that he would pick the fight with you. You've already been in my office several times this year for similar incidents…not to mention the notes were still on the ground when the three of us left. In your story you did not even mention that part. Alex wouldn't have ripped his own class materials for no reason. Because of this major detail you left out, your whole story is void, so I have no choice but to take Alex's side as the definite truth."

I let out a sigh of relief. The tension fled from my shoulders. I was back in good form.

"Not only have you harassed a fellow classmate," he continued, "but you also lied to an authority figure."

He paused for a second, waiting for Rasheed's response. He had none.

"For that reason alone, I should have you expelled… but lucky for you we have a protocol to follow."

He pulled another set of files from his desk drawers and drew a single pink slip. He then reached for the student handbook at the far end of his desk. I leaned forward in my seat to watch him as he switched his focus from the book to the paper. I wasn't exactly sure what he was doing, but I didn't care. The case was ruled in my favor.

"Rasheed, direct your attention here if you will."

He slid the form along with a pen across his desk to where Rasheed and I were sitting.

"This form states that you violated Student Code 23, Section One, 'Endangering a fellow Student's well-being' and Student Code 34, Section Three, 'Damage to Student Property.' As for your punishment, the equivalent is two weeks of afterschool detention and one month behavioral probation."

He was now twirling a spare pen in his hand.

"So I need you to sign here saying that you accept this punishment…"

He pointed to the blank line on the page with his pen, but Rasheed didn't budge.

"Unless of course you want to contest my judgment. If you feel that way, by all means do so."

The principal's eyes lit up as he watched Rasheed, waiting for his response. By the expression on Rasheed's face, I could tell he was unwilling, but he had no other choice. He gnashed his teeth as he gripped the pen in his right hand. As his hand drew closer and closer it became more apparent that he was only seconds away from signing his life away for the next two weeks…and I liked it. I think Mr. Turner did too. It looked like he was actually smiling. When the pen pressed against the paper, he flashed a cynical grin…but it was only for a brief second. Rasheed still needed to sign off on it. And he realized this.

"So, what will it be, Mr. Robins?"

Rasheed looked up and was confronted by a piercing stare.

"We don't have all day…Mr. Rogers has a class to attend…as do you, unless you'd rather spend the day with me, that is." He was grinning again.

"Time's ticking."

He tapped his watch as he chuckled.

Rasheed opened his mouth as if he were about to say something but instead of hearing his voice, I heard the pen scribbling in its place.

"Good…I'm glad we came to an understanding. All I need you to do now is to get it signed by your parents and bring it back tomorrow morning so I can file it. You'll start your detention next week, so in the meantime you can make arrangements for transportation and what not."

Rasheed folded up the slip and put it in his pocket and walked out the door. I began to get up, but Mr. Turner stopped me.

"One second Mr. Rogers…close the door."

What could he possibly want from me?

CHAPTER 4

ON THE JUST AND UNJUST

I shut the door behind me and returned to my seat.

"You know...what you did here today was a good thing. You shouldn't feel bad for what you did...Rasheed deserved it, and you owe it to yourself to stand up to him, as you said earlier. I know I mentioned that he had been to my office before...but while he was in my office on several occasions, he would never get the punishment he deserved. You see, the problem I've been having lately is that the bullies aren't getting the punishment they deserve because the kids aren't speaking out against them. I bring them in the office and they dilute the story because they're afraid it will come back to hurt them in the end...but you were different. You actually told me what happened back there...and I appreciate it."

"Thanks...it was nothing really. It was just something I felt I had to do."

"Exactly! We need more students like you."

"I agree, sir."

"It's a shame though; really it is…you know I could use someone like you."

I was puzzled.

"How so, sir?"

"Well, you see throughout the school I have certain students who act as my eyes on the grounds…I can't be everywhere at once, so these students relay what goes on to me. Don't worry, these students' names are protected and as long as you are discreet no one will know about it. How do you think I know what happened this morning? One of your classmates told me of course. It's a simple system really…if you see a problem with students, just slip away and report it to me."

"So you want me to spy on students for you?"

"No, not *spy*, just observe…I understand that you don't exactly know how to react to what I'm telling you right now, but please take the time to consider."

He was right. I really didn't understand what was going on. I didn't even know they had things like this at school. I needed some time to think this through.

"Will do, sir."

"Oh, and Alex take this."

He pulled out another slip and filled it out.

"Here…it's a slip describing what happened today. Hopefully your teacher won't count your missing assignment against you."

"Thanks."

He handed me the slip. I folded it up and walked toward the door.

"If you need anything, you know where I am. I hope next time we'll meet on different terms."

"Sure."

I walked out the office and pulled out the note.

To whom it may concern:

Today Alex had business to attend to in my office regarding another student. This student ripped up Alex's assignment and was dealt with accordingly. If you have any questions, feel free to drop by my office.

Thank you,

Eric Turner

I folded the note and put it back in my pocket. The bell had already rung so it was no use rushing to class. I still couldn't believe this was happening. I didn't know if I should work for him or not. It wasn't like I had anything to lose. If I did work for Mr. Turner, I knew for a fact that he'd keep Rasheed off my back…but being a rat would cause me to lose the trust of my classmates. I needed some more time to think this through. One thing I did know was I needed to stay on the principal's good side. I'd never been to the principal's office, but after living through it, I didn't ever want to do it again. I hadn't even been in the wrong, but just watching what Rasheed went through was enough for me to keep it that way. I didn't like the way the principal operated. He was so calm but, at the same time, on edge. I really couldn't read him. He also had an *atmosphere* about him. I don't know… maybe I was over-reacting. He was just a principal, after all.

During my classes I found myself thinking about Mr. Turner's offer, more so during history class. When I first walked in the room, everything was fine; but then reality struck when Rasheed entered the room. It wouldn't have been so bad if he sat a couple of seats away from me, but he sat directly behind me, and to top that off, Sheldon was off to his side as well. Perfect, right? I could hear Rasheed and Sheldon murmuring about what had happened this morning. I couldn't make out the words though. So I didn't know if they were planning their next move or finally deciding to leave me alone; regardless, sitting directly in front of my arch nemesis wasn't exactly the best of places to be. I wished the teacher would just change the seating arrangements. *Alphabetical seating sucks…ha! God definitely has a sick sense of humor.*

"You know you're dead, right?" My thoughts were interrupted by a voice.

Mr. Turner's offer was looking pretty good right now.

I tried my best to tune them out and focus on the lesson, but it was no use. Whenever I thought they had given up, they would somehow make their presence known, whether it was trying to steal my book sack or flicking the back of my neck with a finger. They wouldn't let me divert my attention elsewhere. Occasionally the teacher would look over with a confused expression. She thought she heard something. I seriously think all teachers are clueless…hardly anything gets done through them when it comes to this.

"Is everything OK back there?"

"Yes ma'am."

So clueless…*of course not…I'm virtually in a hostage situation. Can you not see that?* At least now that she said something, she brought attention to this area of the room. That quieted them down a bit. When the bell rang, I made sure they left before I did—a good while before me. I took my time packing my books. As I packed I heard the teacher call out from the doorway.

"Remember the test next class! Study hard; it's not going to be easy."

Great…a test. I didn't even know what we had done this class. I was too busy trying to stay alive.

The rest of the students began to leave the room once it was clear she had finished the announcements. I looked up from my desk to see if Rasheed and Sheldon were in my range of vision. They were nowhere in sight.

Good.

I zipped up my bag and headed out the door. I poked my head out the door to check if it was safe to come out.

All clear.

For the rest of the day, my time spent outside of class was a game of cat and mouse. It wasn't that bad really. I just had to make it to my next class without being spotted. It wasn't like Rasheed had my schedule or anything. While I was in class, I was safe, so I didn't actually mind going. Life was easier there…and so much simpler. All I had to do was listen to the teacher and take notes. It was better than how things were outside of class. In class I could concentrate on my schoolwork and leave everything else behind me. It was a good feeling and a great way to end the day. It brought peace to me. It's sad though, that in moments like these, time goes by the fastest. It's always like that for the things you enjoy.

Yeah…English is definitely my favorite class. In the past it helped me focus my thoughts on days like this. Every day toward the end of class, our teacher would give us about twenty minutes or so to write down what had happened to us that day and how it made us feel. Then she would ask us in the end if we would change it, and how. She told me once that sometimes it's just better to write things down…that it brings healing to the soul. She was right. You feel a lot better when you pour out emotions, especially on paper. I was looking forward to that moment today. I needed to get some things off my chest. Maybe if I wrote things out I would get a better outlook on what I should do. It usually worked; it shouldn't be any different today.

As the teacher lectured, I found myself watching the clock.

2:00 P.M.

We should be wrapping up soon. The evening announcements come on around two fifteen. I began to tap my pen eagerly as I watched the time tick down.

"Today, class, we're going to do things a little differently. Instead of free writing, I'm going to give you a topic for you to write on…now that we're well into the semester, I want you to look back at the situations you've been in and tell me, if you could change one thing this school year, what would it be? I know ten minutes isn't enough time to write something like this, so I'm going to make it your final paper for the school year. I just wanted to let you know ahead of time, because you, class, have a lot of thinking to do. It has to be two pages double spaced with a full heading."

I could write you four pages right now, I thought.

The announcements came on…but I didn't really pay attention to them. I started to think about how the school year was stacking up for me this far into it. I really didn't like it, but it wasn't anything that I placed upon myself. "The rain falls upon the just as well as the unjust," my father used to always tell me when I was little. I was starting to understand why. Life throws curve balls, and you just have to prepare for them. Some you can avoid, but some just happen.

The bell rang, and Mr. Turner dismissed us from the intercom.

"You all have a blessed day."

I packed my bags and headed out of the classroom door, only to find myself floating in a sea of students. Everyone was doing their own evening ritual. I saw outcasts horse playing near the lockers, athletes getting their gear together. The usual. I even saw some kid reaching for his leftover change that someone had stolen from him. If anyone of them were asked that same question for English, they would all have a good story. When you got down to it, we all had regrets, and we all wished we could do things a little differently. But sometimes things just didn't turn out the way you wanted.

As I navigated through the hall, I saw Devan getting his books ready. I asked myself, *How did it get this far? We used to be the best of friends—not even a year ago…but now we're like this. What happened?*

We exchanged eye contact for a brief second, but then he closed his locker door and broke it off.

What happened?

He slung his book sack over his shoulder and walked off.

It wasn't long before I found my answer.

As he left the building, I noticed that he was getting wet. It was raining.

Funny how things work.

When I got back from school, I went up to my room, shut my door, and plopped on my bed. I folded my hands under my head as I watched the ceiling fan make its rotations. I heard thunder outside. It was still raining, a little heavier than it was before. I turned my head and watched the rain fall against the screen door. It reminded me of small little drums as it tapped against the glass. It was relaxing. I watched as the droplets raced down the screen, scooping up others along the way. It had been awhile since I took time to appreciate the rain. When I was younger, I used to spend my time during car rides watching the rain pour down in storms like these. It always had a soothing affect on me.

A bolt of lightning flashed, followed by a thunder clap. The house shook.

That one was close, I thought. I turned my head away from the screen and looked up at the ceiling again.

I heard a knock at my door.

"It's open."

It was Mom. Her head was pressed against the door as she opened it.

"Everything OK?"

"Fine."

"OK…the storm's supposed to get worse through the night. On the news they said there might be an outage."

"OK."

She gently closed the door.

I gazed up at the fan again. When it rained I really didn't want to do anything. It was perfect nap weather… probably why everyone liked thunderstorms.

As I watched the fan swirl above me, my eyes began to get heavier. I was getting drowsier and drowsier with each passing rotation. The constant tapping from the rain acted as a sedative. My breaths were coming slower, and I was beginning to lose track of time. My mind began to wander as I slipped further away from consciousness. Even with my eyes closed, the lightning still lit my field of vision. The rain was getting harder. I could hear the trees whipping the sides of the house from outside.

Another thunderclap; the furniture raddled.

I looked at the clock. "12:00" repeatedly flashed in red digital numerals. I must have dozed off. I reached in my pocket for my phone. I clicked the side to find the time. It read 10:42 p.m.

I was still drowsy, and the day was virtually over—no point in waking up again. I closed my eyes and tried to go back to sleep, but images of what had happened today found a way onto the black canvas of my mind, and then my mind began to wander. It seemed like I had a lot of unaddressed questions that needed to be taken care of. Drifting back to school, I remembered Ms. Barrel asking us what we would change so far if we had the chance. If I could change one thing, what would it be? Was it even smart to think like that? Everything happens for a reason, right? So, why change a thing? If everything has a purpose, then this does too…or not. People don't need a reason to do anything. They act on impulse. I learned that today. People don't need a reason to act the way they do. They just do it. Maybe I'm wrong. Maybe there's a meaning behind all of this. Whatever…I didn't want to think about this anymore. There was no use thinking about it.

I rolled on my side and tried to go back to sleep. *I'll sort it all out tomorrow.*

I promise.

Those were my last thoughts that night. Somehow I managed to go to sleep during the storm. The rest of the week passed over just like the storm…and the others were quick behind it. Not too much trouble had gone down between Rasheed and me since then. He was on thin ice due to another mishap with another kid. That night when I said there was no use thinking about my problems anymore, I meant it, so the next morning I decided to take action.

I finally went and talked to Mr. Turner and he gladly offered me a spot on his board. It wasn't that bad. Nothing really changed for the most part and it wasn't really that hard to do. He would give us the name of a student, and we kept an eye on him. Most of the time, it wasn't bullies. Made sense though. There was no need to throw me in the line of fire. It usually ended up that the ones being picked on were the ones we watched. It was a good feeling. It felt like I was finally moving on with my life. The past was the past and I was free.

CHAPTER 5

A SECOND CHANCE; STEPPING FROM THE SHADOWS

"You called, sir?"

I was in his office bright and early; it was at least seven o'clock. Yesterday Mr. Turner had told me to come to school early for an assignment he needed help with. I wondered what it was.

"Yes," he said. He was sitting at his desk with a student already in his office. The student was big for his age but also well built. He was probably the subject of this conversation...

"Alex, let me introduce you to our newest student, Nader Johnson.

Nader stood up and extended his hand for me to shake. The tips of his fingers were coarse. He was either a very hard worker or a musician.

"Nader is here to finish up the rest of the school year with us. Hopefully he will choose to finish the rest of his high school career with us as well. Now, Alex, what I called you here for today is I want you to show Nader around the campus…get to know him…you know, help ease him into how things work around here."

"No problem."

"Good. Just drop him off at my office when the bell rings. He starts tomorrow."

"OK."

Nader and I walked out his office and began to explore the campus grounds. I showed him the library, the cafeteria, the gym, the different buildings, and even the location of his classes on his schedule. He was a cool guy. While I showed him around, he started to talk a bit about himself. Turns out he was of Jamaican and Spanish decent. His parents grew up out of the country but decided to move here when he was eight. He had no problems with it, but his mother only spoke her native language. I would have thought he was something else, judging by his complexion and hairstyle. And it turned out he *was* a musician. It might not be too bad hanging out with this Nader guy after all. I dropped him off back at the office before the bell rang, just as directed. I would have to see him tomorrow as well, but I really didn't mind. This could be the start of an interesting friendship.

As I walked out the door, he called out and stopped me. "Hey, Alex!"

I turned and looked behind me.

"I was wondering if we could hang out later today, after school."

"Sure. I don't see why not."

"Cool. See you there…here's my address," he said as he wrote it down on a folded piece of paper and handed it to me.

"Of course."

I put it in my pocket and walked away.

The rest of the day was over before I knew it. Math was easy, I aced my history test, and english was a breeze as always. That evening I met Nader at his house. Surprisingly it wasn't too far from school. He lived in a pretty nice neighborhood. Most of the houses were two stories. When I got there he was already outside.

"Glad you found it!"

I laughed. "It wasn't that hard. I've been living here my whole life. I know how to get around."

"Ready to see the house?"

"Sure."

He escorted me through the first floor of the house; then we stopped at the kitchen.

"Do you want something to eat?"

"No, I'm good."

"Thirsty? We have orange juice, apple juice, grape juice—"

"Any soft drinks?" I interrupted.

"No, but we have water."

"No thanks…I'll pass."

He looked disappointed. Maybe I should have taken him up on his offer.

"Hey, let me show you something upstairs real quick!"

"Sure."

On the way upstairs, he turned backward and began to talk to me again. "You know how I told you that I liked to play music? Well, check this out."

He opened the door at the end of the hallway.

"This is where all the magic happens, as they like to say."

He had his own studio. It was pretty cool. It had a bunch of instruments and equipment scattered about the room. Some were covered up, while others were just on the floor. It wasn't the greatest, but at least it was something.

"Alex."

"Hmmm?"

"Do you play?"

He had a guitar in his hand.

"No. But my brother Jason always wanted to play...he took a couple of lessons."

"Oh...did you ever want to play anything when you were younger?"

"Just the drums...my uncle taught me a bit one summer. I tried the piano a bit too, but I was no good."

"That's cool...it takes courage to play, man."

He put the guitar down and walked deeper into the room.

"So what do you play? Well, besides the guitar."

He laughed. "Harmonica, sitar, flute, some drums, and of course the guitar. Oh, and this."

He motioned me to follow him as he walked toward a piece of equipment covered in a blue plastic tarp.

"It's old, but it's still quite the beaut...check it out."

He removed the tarp.

"It's a beat-making machine. This is how it all started, actually."

He dusted the keys while he talked.

"Yeah, when I first moved here, I didn't really have any friends, so after school I wouldn't hang out with friends or go to the movies, nothing like that. I just sat up here and made music. It was all I had. I always stuck to myself, but one day, for a talent show at school, I performed a song I worked on over the summer. Lyrics 'n' all, and they all liked it. For a moment everyone in the room came together. I liked that feeling, and I wanted more of it. I liked the way it felt, but more importantly, the way it made everyone else feel. Music can bring a family together, music can mend a broken heart, it can save a marriage, it can make two people realize how much they need each other. It can do all these things…but most importantly, it brings people together. You know, out of everything in the world we have now, I think music brings us closest together. That's why that day when I was on stage, I decided to be a musician. I experienced it first hand, and I want to spend the rest of my life giving that feeling to others."

He stopped for a moment. "Ha-ha…sorry, I didn't mean to get carried away like that."

"It's OK. You like what you do. No shame in that. It's good that you found your passion so young. A lot of people are still searching."

"Yeah, I guess you're right. But people tell me all the time I should be more realistic with my goals. I guess I'm a dreamer."

He quickly changed the subject. "Anyway…it's finally ready."

His eyes lit up with anticipation. "I had to wait awhile, but it's finally ready. This was my first beat-making machine."

"That's cool. I always thought being a producer would be cool…never actually seen one of these in person though."

"Yeah, they're amazing…go ahead and try it. It's easier than it looks. You'll do fine."

"Ha-ha. I really shouldn't; maybe next time."

"Come on! Live a little."

"Hmmm…I'll make a deal with you…if you introduce yourself to fifteen people tomorrow at school, I'll try it out."

"No way!"

"Ha-ha, what happened to live a little?"

"But that's different!"

"Ha! I'll be satisfied with ten! Heck, if you do five, I'll record a whole album with you."

"Deal! You know I'm going to hold you to that!"

"By all means."

We shook and made it official.

"Oh, and I forgot…you have to get their numbers too, so I know you didn't just make everything up."

"We already shook!"

"Scared?"

"No, I'll do it!"

"Fine," I said, smiling. "It's settled then. Tomorrow you have to greet five people *and* get their numbers for proof."

"We shook again and made it final."

That day I really didn't mind making that deal with Nader. He was shy, and this was a good way to break him out of his shell, plus I didn't mind making music. I really didn't do anything around the house anyway, so I could use a few tips. This could be the start of an interesting friendship.

I woke up. The alarm was vibrating on the side of my desk.

Six thirty already?

As much as I hated it, I had to get up. Today was Nader's first day. Yesterday I told him that I would meet him at the front of the school before the bell rang. So it was time to get dressed. I sat up in my bed for a while, just to wake up, and looked out my window. The sun was just now coming up. Light from the rays pierced between the blinds and dimly lit the room. As the morning went by, I watched the light slither from my bed to my door, lighting up the hallway. I think that was God's way of telling me it was time to get out of bed. I scooted to the edge of my bed and hung my feet over the side. I slowly moved my feet onto the wooden tiles one by one. The cold sensation always woke me up in the mornings. I dragged my feet across the floor as I wiped the crust away from my eyes. I stumbled into my closet and fished out my uniform. I had ironed it and hung it up the night before, so it wasn't too much of a hassle getting dressed.

By the time I got downstairs, morning drowsiness was a thing of the past. I made a light breakfast and was out the door in a flash. I left with a piece of toast in my mouth. I had a feeling that today would be a good day.

As I approached the school gates, I saw Nader arriving to school as well. His parents were dropping him off. He was too far off for me to get his attention, so I just let him go. He didn't seem too bad from what I saw. Hopefully all would go well today. I picked up the pace and followed after him to the front entrance.

"Nader!" I yelled as I ran across the schoolyard. He stopped and staggered a bit.

"Wait up!"

I brushed the sweat off my brow and hunched over as I tried to catch my breath. He turned around and walked toward me.

"You know, I do martial arts as well...you should take some classes with me."

I barely had enough breath to respond. "Ha-ha. Shut up...you ready for your first day?"

"Yeah, might as well be...it's going to happen whether or not I want it to happen."

"You know, you're starting to sound like me. Come on, let's go inside. It won't be long before the bell rings."

"You're delusional."

"Whatever."

We walked into the school. The halls were already saturated. Students were dispersed everywhere, attending to their own matters as usual.

"Hey...you remember your locker number?"

"Yeah, 1311."

"You should pack your books for the day right now. It makes it easier to transfer classes that way."

"It doesn't matter. It's not like I'm looking forward to class."

"You know, I was just kidding about yesterday. You don't have to do all that on your first day if you don't want to. You should take your time to ease into the community first. I wasn't exactly an open book my first couple weeks at school, so it's understandable."

"Yeah..."

"But don't worry, you'll do fine. Everyone's pretty civil around here."

As I said that, I couldn't help but think about how things were at first for me, dealing with Rasheed and everything else. It gave me a headache just thinking about it. A familiar sound in the background brought me back to reality.

The bell rang and Nader was already walking off. It didn't take long before the morning rush was in full effect. He was soon lost in a sea of people and the distance between us was growing as the tide pushed me back. But I was determined to give him one last piece of advice. It would give me peace about the whole situation. I cuffed my hands and yelled across the hall.

"Nader!"

I saw his head turn back in the midst of all the commotion.

"You'll do fine, but if anyone gives you trouble, just let me know! I'll handle 'em."

He turned around and gave me a thumbs-up as he walked away in the crowd. I watched him as he faded into the background.

The rest of the day I didn't worry about him much. I knew things would turn out for the best with him. Even with the anticipation in the back of my mind, the day still flew by. I found myself in the same position as always, twirling my pencil, looking at the clock in my last class. The last five minutes was always the worst part. By then everything was said and done, so there was just awkward silence. I watched the time wind down, second by second. I was eager to spring from my desk and finish the rest of my day. I had things to do, people to see. I wondered how Nader's first day had gone. I needed to catch up with him as soon as the bell rang. Hopefully it hadn't been too bad.

Overhead, I heard static from the intercom. The evening announcements were underway. *Just a little bit longer,* I thought. A voice sounded from the box.

"Good evening, students."

The principal went on. I didn't care much about what he was saying. All I wanted to hear was that bell ring. As I looked around the classroom from my desk, I could see that for a brief moment everyone in the class shared a universal consciousness. Everyone, including the teacher, was already prepared to go but was waiting on the final dismissal. We all were on the edge of our seats, as Mr. Turner began to wrap things up. Then he finally dismissed us.

"Have a blessed day."

And with those words, the silence was broken. New life rushed into the room once again. Students stockpiled at the exits, rushing to get on with the rest of their afternoons. I sat down. I wanted to go too but, it wasn't that much of an issue…just because the school year was coming to a close didn't mean you had to get reckless. Rules are rules, regardless of the situation. After the rush several other students and I left, followed by the teacher.

Great, now to find Nader. I thought. *He shouldn't be hard to find. It's only his first day… he'll most likely be near the office where he was when we first met.* With that in mind, I made my way to the front office.

Nader was there in all his glory. From afar I noticed him talking with two other students. He had a full-grown smile running across his face. That was a good sign. After awhile the two guys walked away; he noticed me from the corner of his eye and met me halfway.

"So, how'd it go?" I asked enthusiastically.

"Great!" he said. I could tell he was full of energy. He was beaming through his actions. I was happy for him. I watched him as he continued his story. As he told it, he couldn't sit still. His hands were everywhere, and he was pacing in front of me. "Yeah, I met some real cool people today. It wasn't bad at all. I told them about my music, and then the rest was history!"

I laughed. "Well, I guess that makes you more popular than me, Nader."

His facial expression changed. "What's that suppose to mean?"

"Nothing." I looked at him with a blank stare.

"Hey, don't hate because I'm climbing the ranks!" I laughed again. "Yeah?"

"Yeah, and you're coming along with me!" He pulled out a sheet of paper from his pocket. It didn't take me long to realize what he was grabbing for, but I was still in denial. I watched in anticipation as he flaunted the folded paper in front of my face and began to unravel it slowly. "It's exactly what you think it is." He shoved the paper in front of my face. "Count them out. Five numbers!" He slid his finger down the list. "One-two-three-four-*five*!"

I scanned over the paper repeatedly in disbelief. It wasn't a bad thing, just unexpected. If anything, I was proud of him for conquering his fears…we could all learn a lesson or two from this guy.

"So, you know what that means, right?"

A smile cracked on my face. "We're making an album together."

He nodded. "That's right…and I've already put the word out." Everything else I was cool with, but that little tidbit got me a little worried. I thought it would just be a little project for me and him to work on, but it became apparent that he had something bigger in mind.

"What's the matter?" He read the expression on my face and could see that I was having second thoughts.

"Alex, you should take your own advice. I've noticed that you yourself really don't hang out with many people either. You always seem to just be in the shadows. I don't see why though. You told me yourself that I needed to take chances and live a little. I made five friends today, plus interest, because of the push you gave me. Now it's time to push yourself. Why not make the album? Why not go for it? You only live once, and if you pass up the opportunity now, you'll only regret it later. Why not take a chance? The worst that could happen is no one likes it. But at least we tried, right?"

As much as I wanted to agree with him, part of me couldn't. But he was right. All this time, I'd been hiding in the shadows. Because of what had happened earlier in the school year, I had become more reserved and kept to myself. It guaranteed that it wouldn't happen again, but at the same time, it forced me to be less social. Sure I would associate with my classmates, some more than others, but all in all I kept to myself to avoid being put in that situation again. I played a pretty good game. I had convinced everyone else, even myself, but not Nader. He hadn't even known me for a week yet, but still he was a hundred percent right.

He extended his hand toward me. "Are you in or are you out?"

I guess it's true when they say God puts people in your life for a reason…and I thought it was about time I stepped out from the shadows. Hiding was no use—nothing there anyway.

"Yeah, I'm in," I responded.

He smiled and answered back. "Good, I thought I lost you for a minute back there…but now that we're on the same terms, we need to get this album underway ASAP. I already promised them it would be a hit, and you have to give the people what they want."

"OK, so when are we starting?"

"Right now…we're going to go to my house and get things started."

Even though I said I wanted to commit, I still tried to talk my way out it.

"I have other pla—"

"Live a little!" He cut me off and grabbed me by the wrist. "You're coming with me, whether you like it or not!" He practically dragged me from the school parking lot to his house.

When we got there, we immediately went upstairs to the studio.

"Both of my parents work late, so we won't have to worry about noise."

"Cool. So what type of CD are we making?"

"You said you liked the beat-making machine, so we can produce some instrumentals. Come over here. I'll show you how it's done."

I walked over to the machine as he started it up.

From that day forward, every day after school, Nader and I reported to his house to make music together. He was a real good hype man too. As the weeks rolled by, he spread the word about our latest endeavors, leaking tracks to students and dropping release dates for singles.

Even during the summer, when school was out, he kept fans up-to-date on social networking sites. He even made a page that let guests sample our music. Our reputation was starting to rise, and our listeners grew anxious for our official album to drop. I remember during the summer he updated the page saying that it would drop our sophomore year. It was a good decision considering that once we were back at school they could put a face to the name. It would start a buzz and would be a good way to start off the new semester.

Originally we did this just for fun, to get our names out, to prove something to ourselves. Whatever. But it was slowly becoming something more. I had my regrets, but then again, in the end you always do. They say hindsight is always 20/20. I couldn't agree more.

CHAPTER 6

WAS IT WORTH IT? I HOPE YOU'RE HAPPY IN THE END

The morning before the first day of school, we were supposed to meet outside the gates. We burned more than enough copies the night before to distribute to our class, and it was Nader's job to bring them to school. I took it upon myself to show up early. We were supposed to meet at 7:20, but I decided to show at 7:10. A couple minutes later, I saw a car coming in the distance. It was Nader. I remembered his parents' cars from all the visits over the summer. I didn't know what he told them, but they seemed to drop him off in a hurry. I watched as the car sped away and then turned to him.

"Got the CDs?"

He flashed his gym bag that was tucked away at his side. It was illegal to carry any multimedia of any kind on school grounds, so this was the method of choice by all the students that went there. Even cell phones weren't allowed on the grounds till after hours.

"Good."

The plan was simple. All we had to do was wait for school to be out and hand out the CDs. Nothing complicated. The biggest issue would be the wait. Remember when you were a kid and you'd count down the days till Christmas? The closer it came, the longer the days seemed, especially the night before. I would be in pure agony watching the clock, trying to ease the sensation, but it only made things worse. It wasn't any better with TV either. All they had on were Christmas specials and those only made me fantasize about how it would be when that day would finally come. Now, picture that but multiply it by a hundred. That was how I felt.

A tap on my shoulder shifted me back to reality.

"Don't worry, I got this. I'll hand them out after school. Hell, maybe in between classes if the timing's right."

"I wouldn't. You know how teachers are. If you get caught, then they'll confiscate the bag. How's it gonna look when the principal sees me in the office with contraband material? I work for the man."

As I tried to reason with him, I noticed his eyes begin to squint. "Correction, you *used* to work for him." He had a snarl in his voice. "He hasn't heard from you in months. He probably forgot about you."

He was becoming more aggressive. His head was only inches from my face.

"Why would you go back to that anyway? So you can deal with retards like Malcolm? Huh? Do you want that? Do you really want that?"

It was a really bad move to bring up Malcolm. If anything it was a low blow. By now you're probably wondering exactly who Malcolm was, and I'll be glad to fill you in.

Not too long after I met Nader, Mr. Turner called me over to watch over another student. According to his transcript, this particular student's grades had steadily decreased after his arrival. We knew he had a learning disability, but Mr. Turner also suspected that bullying was in the mix. He wasn't in any of my classes, so the only time I could see him was during lunch. I used to split my days during the week, eating with Malcolm or Nader. Eventually the three of us started to share a table together.

Just from interacting with him, I could tell Malcolm was a little shaken. Private schools didn't have a special education program, so they put him in all remedial classes, along with the less proficient students. That was the best they could do, but even still he struggled. When he talked he often stuttered, but I didn't judge him...I never did. He was only human, after all. But for some reason, the other kids didn't seem to get that. He was just like the rest of us. He laughed, he cried, he had his ups and downs, just like everyone else.

Mr. Turner was right about how his grades were slipping, but it didn't take me long to figure out why. One day on the way to lunch, I saw two kids harassing him, calling him a retard and playing cruel jokes on him. I didn't know how I didn't catch it sooner, and even today I beat myself for it. He was in a corner, and they were hitting him with sticks, calling him everything they could think of. I didn't know the full story, but one thing I did find out was just how big his heart was.

After I got the authorities, I dusted him off and asked him if he was OK. He had cuts above his eyes, and his pants were ripped, but still he replied with a smile on his face. After everything was settled at lunch, I asked him why they'd hit him. He put down his food and just looked at me. He was teary eyed. I shouldn't have asked such a stupid question. He didn't even know why they hit him. He broke the silence and mustered a sentence.

"They…they sa-said it was because I was stu-stupid." A single tear rolled down the side of his cheek. "D-do you think I'm stupid?" I looked at him while the reality of what he said sunk in. "You don't think I'm stupid d-do you? Tears began to well up in my face.

"No…no, Malcolm, I don't."

He smiled at me.

"I don't think you're stupid at all. You shouldn't let people tell you who you are. Remember that. A couple years back, I was in the same situation as you. I thought I was stupid. Everyone called me dumb, retard, anything they could think of…I tried not to listen to them, but eventually I started to believe them. I would go home and cry. I thought I was worthless. Even my own brother lost faith in me. But you know what I did? I put all those feelings aside, and I relied on me. You define yourself, Malcolm. Remember that…it took me long enough to come to terms with that realization, but it's the truth."

As I continued to speak, I tried my best to hold my tears in. I tried as hard as possible to keep my voice strong.

"You can be whatever you want to be. Don't let anyone take your dreams away from you. You're not stupid. No matter what they say. You're not stupid, you're not ugly, you're not slow, you are you, and you define who you are,

Malcolm. Don't let anyone else tell you otherwise. Those boys out there don't know you. Do you know why they pick on you?"

He shook his head.

"They do it because you're different. That's why they pick on you; that's why they picked on me; it's because we're different. But that doesn't mean we should stop being who we are. Someone once told me we are who we say we are. Do you believe that Malcolm?"

"Y-yes, I do."

"So what are you? Are you stupid?"

I stared at him with tears in my eyes. I was trying my best not to lose my composure.

"Are you?" My voice cracked.

"No," he replied weakly.

I wanted him to say it like he meant it. Not just for me but for himself. It wasn't the first time he'd seen this and it wouldn't be the last. If I could give him anything, I just wanted him to know what he was; he was human.

"I can't hear you! Are you stupid?"

"No."

"Are you stupid!?"

"*No!*"

"*No, I am not stupid!*" Tears were flowing down his face as he preached his exclamation.

"That's right, you aren't. Now the next time they say you can't do something, I want you to tell them that. You're not stupid. And next time you begin to doubt yourself, I want you to remind yourself that you're not stupid, OK? You got that?"

He nodded and lunged over the cafeteria table and hugged me. He was crying, but it was tears of joy.

"Th-thank you, Alex"

"No. Thank you."

I learned a lot from Malcolm that day, and from that point on, our friendship only blossomed. Out of all that he was, the one thing I admired most about Malcolm was his big heart. No matter what he went through, I always saw him with a smile on his face, and while being his friend, I tried my best to copy that habit of his. Whether it was a bad test score or kids messing with him, by the end of the day, he would be smiling. He always used to tell me not to worry, that things would work out in the end. Sometimes it was hard to believe him, but he had a point. Everything does work out in the end. Whether it's to our liking or not is a different matter; but everything that starts has to end. Unfortunately that same rule applied to our friendship.

During finals week Mr. Turner informed me after school that Malcolm didn't get the required grades to pass for the year. The rule was that if you failed more than two classes, you couldn't come back the following school year. He had failed three classes. I couldn't do anything but accept it. It was a heartbreaking moment, but in the end it turned out to be a blessing in a curse.

On a Wednesday soon after that, I still hadn't written my English final. The topic was pick one thing we could change that happened to us, and why. That night when I got home, I decided to write about my friendship with Malcolm. The one thing I wished I could have changed was to have known him before all this happened. In such a little amount of time, he taught me so much, and I resented the fact that he was leaving us so soon. Looking back at it, I honestly think he was fully capable. He was a smart kid. People just got to him. If people start calling you something, pretty soon you begin to believe it. If they had ignored his speech impediment, he would probably have done well enough to stay.

During the summer I kinda forgot about him at times. Nader was a good distraction, but at other times I always felt that I could have done more to help him. That, somehow, it was my fault. He left me with a good tip though. He was right: everything always works out in the end... I just have to keep telling myself that. I hope he's OK wherever he is.

⁂

"Hey! I'm sorry! I said I'm sorry! You don't have to keep staring at me like that!" Nader waved his hand across my face. "I didn't mean those things I said. I'm sorry...I just get carried away sometimes. I was in the moment."

"It's not too good to live in the moment."

"Al, you need to li—"

"Live a little?"

"Whatever..."

As I turned my back to him, the bell rang. "I'm going to class. Do whatever you like with the CDs...I don't care."

By lunch time I was already starting to hear the buzz about the early release. By the end of the day, people were coming up to me telling me how good a job we did. I took it with a grain of salt, but Nader was ecstatic. On the way home from school, I told him that I wasn't coming over. I was still aggravated by what he'd said earlier.

"What do you mean you're not coming over?" He cut me off by walking backward ahead of me.

"You're in the way."

"Are you still mad?"

"It was the first day of school. Don't you think I should go home? My parents are gonna want to know what happened."

"That can wait…you sleep there. You should ditch them and come with me. Did you see how everyone was today? They loved it! We need to start working on a follow up ASAP. We need to capitalize!"

I kept walking. "Maybe tomorrow…I'm tired."

The next day was the same routine. Nader begged me to spend time after school and work on a new release, but I declined. The first CD had just been to prove something to ourselves; it wasn't meant to become my new pastime. I was content with where things were, but he was growing impatient. As the days rolled on, our fame began to decline, and we were becoming old news. The students had more important things to focus on. School had just begun, and everyone had adopted their own agenda trying to stay ahead of the game. No one was going to wait for another album to drop. Eventually Nader got tired of waiting on me and decided to announce a second project without my consent. I had no idea about it until people starting asking me about release dates. I never took the time to go see Nader and ask him about it. I figured eventually he would come after me and fill me in. It took him a week to relay the information to me.

I finally got my chance to speak to him, when he stopped me in the halls one afternoon.

"We're fading out, Al. We can make a comeback, but I can't do it alone. Let's give this another go," Nader said.

"Word on the street is you already got something up your sleeve."

"Oh that? I just created a buzz, you know, something to keep their mouths going. But I got nothing, so we need to do this together."

"Are you insane? Why won't you let this go? You're making this bigger than it actually is. You gave away those tapes for free. It's not like you're a rapper. It was for fun, Nader, but the fun's over with. How are your grades? You're obsessing and you need to realize that. Maybe we can do another one during the next break, but for now, just move on. And don't make promises you can't fulfill… people will only be upset in the end."

I didn't mean to make him mad, but that's what happened anyway. He was furious. I just wanted to tell him the truth, but he couldn't handle it.

"I'm going to make that CD with or without you. Just watch."

After he said that, he stormed off. With his departure he left a string of rumors in his wake. Before the end of the day, people were asking me why we'd split, if we were fighting, all kinds of stuff. It even got worse as time progressed.

In the following days, I began to hear more and more rumors. I tried not to let it get to me, but it was kinda hard not to with people asking me about it on sight. The latest propaganda was someone saying a diss track was going to be released about me come Monday because Nader felt that I had betrayed him. My initial reaction to it was that he was just trying to add fuel to the fire. Did he want me to make a track back? If he had any sense, he wouldn't release it. I didn't think an album was something to lose a friendship over. That was Friday.

Over the weekend I started to get worried about his next move, so I tried to call him, but he never picked up.

That weekend I made it my primary focus to get in touch with him. All day Saturday I called his cell phone on the hour every hour, and on Sunday I even went to his house. He wasn't there though; either that or he didn't answer. As the day progressed, I found myself growing more and more anxious. I spent the whole day franticly refreshing our old music page to see if he had any new updates online. I paced my room till midnight to burn time. If he was going to release it Monday, a midnight release was possible. At 12:05 I checked, but nothing was there. I rested easy that night. It would be a long time till I would be able to say that again.

On Monday I woke up a little later than usual because of the night before. It took no time to get ready, and I was out the door relatively quickly. I had to make up for lost time and talk to Nader before school started. I didn't know how he was going to release the CD, so I had to talk it over with him before he got the chance. It wasn't long before I was in the halls of the school, but upon arrival I knew I was too late. When I opened the doors to the hall, the students all looked at me like I was a stranger. I felt their eyes shadow me as I walked toward my locker. Behind me I could hear two of them talking as I entered my combination.

"Is that the kid that the song was about?"

"I think so…yeah, that's definitely him."

"Do you think he knows about it?"

"I don't know…I feel kinda bad for him."

"He's still a fag, anyway…look at him."

I slammed my locker shut and looked at them. One of them just looked at me. The other laughed and walked away.

"What a fag," he said. He was holding his stomach with a forced laugh.

I didn't even know who those two guys were. When had Nader gotten the chance to hand all of the CDs out? The school hadn't even been open for an hour.

I turned and put my back against the locker. Everyone was staring again. A few of the students muffled their laughter; others had a look of pity on their faces. One kid stopped me as I was about to exit.

"Hey."

"Hey."

"You do know what happened, right?"

"Yeah, I know."

"Are going to respond?"

"It's not worth it. It'll only feed the fire. If people are dumb enough to follow this, let them be."

Before he could respond, I slung open the door and quietly walked by him. I sat down on a bench outside the buildings. As students passed, it was the same reaction as the others. Some laughed, some asked me questions, some paid me no mind. Some even quoted verses in my face. Out of all of them, though, I didn't see one physical copy. Not that it even mattered at this point. I tried my best not to let it hamper my mood, but the truth was it was starting to get to me. The day hadn't even started yet, and it was already a catastrophe. I had two options. I could get Mr. Turner involved and have him handle the situation and eradicate Nader, or I could talk to him personally. Honestly it didn't matter anyway. If I talked to the principal, no matter what happened, everyone would still know; and if I talked to Nader, it wouldn't be like he could take back what he had said. The majority of the class had heard it already and even some kids from the other grades.

I rested my head on the palms of my hand and ran my fingers through my hair. Shoes were clicking in the distance against the pavement. I raised my head as the sound got closer.

"You OK, Alex?"

It was one of my teachers.

"Fine…just a rough morning."

"Wake up on the wrong side of the bed?"

"Ha-ha, yeah, something like that." I rubbed the side of my neck.

"Yeah, I'm having one of those mornings too…but I can't let that stop me, can I? You should pack your books; the bell is about to ring."

The teacher leaned in and tapped me on the shoulder. "Don't worry. Things will get better. Just tough it out a bit longer; the rain always passes, so cheer up." He waved goodbye and walked off. I take back what I said awhile back about teachers being clueless.

He had given me good advice, but I wish it were that simple. As I sat on the bench, I wondered what I would tell Nader, what he would tell me. Was there anything he could even say? *He knows what he's done,* I thought. *That's why he hasn't shown his face since.* I sank my head lower between my knees. Was he even going to show up today? Maybe I should go to Mr. Turner. What was done was done…no need to let the situation get worse…*yeah, that's what I'll do.*

The bell rang. I could hear its echo from the inside the buildings around me. An electric chime also sounded for the students still outside.

But first I needed to go to class.

In class nothing really went on. It was still early, so not many people knew about what had happened. Of course some did. Throughout homeroom I heard my name pop up a couple of times from across the room, but I still kept my spirits high. I didn't want to give them a show. My morning was ruined but not my life. This was just one moment of many. I just had to keep reminding myself that. During my second class, I made up my mind that I would see Mr. Turner at lunch. Until then I would just have to hold my tongue. Between classes was the only time I had trouble. I saw the same kids from before talking about me. Did they just think it was cool to join in? Did they even recognize what they're doing?

"Where you going, fag?" one of the students said.

"Is what they say about you true?" the other one called out.

I ignored them and kept walking toward my next class.

"Why aren't you responding? You can say all that smack to Nader over the Internet but not in person?"

That caught my attention. I turned around. "What do you mean?"

"Don't act like you don't know. It's too late for that… come on, let's go."

I watched them as they disappeared together in the hallway.

I walked into the classroom and sat down. During class I couldn't help but wonder what Nader had said. Why would he go so far for something so small? Was our friendship not really worth that much to him? Apparently not.

As I sat in my chair, I could feel my emotions building in my chest. I had to try my best to keep them down. I just had to hold on a bit longer. I thought I would be OK, but I began to remember how I had felt last year. I guess history has a habit of repeating itself. My eyes began to water, but I held back the tears. *I got to focus on my schoolwork,* I thought. *Just a little bit longer.* For the rest of the period, I tried to hold back my tears.

When the bell rang again, it was time for lunch. As I walked down the halls, I heard them chanting names at me. It was hard to walk with my head up when people were constantly trying to force it down. They saw it is as entertainment; I saw it another way. It's hard to recognize someone's pain if you're laughing at it.

"Where you going, fatty? The cafeteria's the other way." I heard one of the students call out. His voice was like a precursor of what was to come. Several others started to join in antagonizing me, in the halls and outside. It didn't matter. No matter where I went, they were behind me.

"When you look down can you even see your toes? It's called a diet, in case you didn't know."

I just kept walking, but still they followed. Wherever I went they were behind me, slinging insults at my back, praying that I'd fall, but I kept moving. No matter how much it hurt me, I couldn't give in. That would only lead to more pain. The further I went, the louder they got. My feet began to get heavier and heavier with every step. I was losing my motivation. My body was getting heavier. It felt like I was carrying my own cross on my shoulders. I had been wrongly accused, and now I was walking with a death sentence on my shoulders. I just wanted it off. I wanted to quit. But I still dragged my feet across the pavement in spite of it all. As I approached the building where

Mr. Turner's office was, the students became silent and went to lunch.

"Let's go before the fatty eats it all."

In the hallway I could see the expressions of the other students. They just watched in silence as I reached out for the door handle. *I could end it all here,* I thought. *Just a little farther.* When I approached the door, I took a moment to pull myself together.

Deep breaths…OK.

"Ms. Bridget?" I knocked on the screen door. I twisted it and walked in.

"Hey, Alex, it's been awhile. How's school been treating you? You OK?"

"Yeah, just a rough day."

"Those first few days can be a doozy…what can I do for you?"

I knew what I had to do, and even though Nader had hurt me, I at least wanted to hear his side of the story. In my hands I held life and death. Now that the moment had finally come, I had trouble figuring out what I actually wanted to do. After all of this, how could I still consider Nader a friend?

"Is Mr. Turner here? I need to speak to him."

"Sorry baby, he stepped out for lunch. Do you want me to deliver a message to him?"

"No, it's OK. I'll stop by later."

"OK. I'll tell him you dropped by…you should go get lunch. They only serve that once around here, you know."

"Thank you…I will."

I turned around and shut the door behind me. Lunch in and of itself would be a whole other issue. I didn't want to face the students again. I took a deep breath and popped my head back into the office.

"Can I eat lunch here today?" It was sad that I was reduced to this. I couldn't even eat in public.

"Sure, honey."

"OK...I'll be right back; just give me a sec."

I closed the door again and walked toward the snack machine outside. As I approached it, I put my hand in my pocket and jingled my change around. Hopefully I had enough. I picked it up and started to count...five... fifteen...twenty...forty-five...seventy...eighty...

Eighty cents. That was enough for something. I scanned the machine and looked for something in my price range. All I could get was a bag of chips. At least it was something. I wasted no time returning to the office. Maybe when the crowd died down, I'd get a bite in before the bell rang. I knocked on the door again.

"Ms. Bridget?"

I cracked it open a bit and walked in.

"Hey, Alex."

I sat in one of the chairs and opened my bag.

"Is that all you're going to eat?"

"I'm on a diet..." As I ate I kept my eye on the clock. The bell was about to ring, and Mr. Turner still hadn't come back.

"Yeah, I don't think he's coming back anytime soon. He went out to lunch with some of the staff. They're probably at a restaurant. It could take a while. I'll tell him you stopped by, so you can rest easy. It seemed to be pretty important if you would eat lunch in here just to see him."

"It's nothing really. I just haven't seen him since school started, that's all. Just wanted to do some catching up. I always used to drop by…it feels kinda bad just leaving cold turkey, ya know?"

"Oh, I understand."

I looked up at the clock again.

"Hey, I have to go. The bell's going to be ringing in a few, so I might as well switch out my books and get a head start on the midday rush. See ya."

Before she had a moment to respond, I rushed out the door. It wouldn't be long until the other students would be leaving the cafeteria. As I made my way out into the hall, I heard a set of footsteps coming from the main entrance in front of the office.

Mr. Turner? I wondered.

I turned around and listened for the steps again.

"Mr. Turner?" I called out.

I heard them again.

"Mr. Turner?" I called out again for him, as I turned the corner.

The footsteps stopped, and I heard a door close toward the center of the hall.

I was almost certain it was him. "Mr. Turner!"

I rushed down the hall and reached for the door knob.

"I need to speak with you for a little while!" I lunged for the doorknob, but before I could grab it, it slowly opened from the other side.

"Nader?"

As the door swung open, we finally met face to face.

A look of amazement flashed across his face. I was the last person he was expecting to see. "Alex?" he said, as he took a step out of the office. Of course he was taken by surprise seeing me. I bet he had checked into school late in hopes of avoiding me. I couldn't say what I wanted to because we were still in front of the door.

"Is everything alright, boys?" Behind Nader I could see Ms. Bridget leaning out from the side of her desk.

"Fine," I told her. "I heard some footsteps in the hall, so I thought Mr. Turner had come back. That's all."

I directed my attention back to Nader. His expression had changed from last time. He had an anxious look on his face. He didn't know if I knew what had happened or not. It was a perfect time to play this to my advantage. I had a plan. I just had to get him away from everyone else.

"What? You look like you've seen a ghost. Come on; let's go before the bell rings. We have to beat the traffic... I hope you ate lunch before you got here. See you later, Ms. Bridget."

I leaned to the side and waved to her and walked out into the hall with Nader. I had to hold his attention, so I stirred up a conversation so he wouldn't notice me scanning our surroundings.

"So. What's up with you? You're just now getting to school. You sick?"

He had a puzzled look on his face. "No, my mom's car broke down this morning so we had to wait till lunch for Dad to drop us off. On top of that, I wanted to stay home because I wasn't feeling too good."

Lying bastard, I thought. I almost gagged. *So you're just going to lie to me in my face? You think I have no idea, huh? You were probably sick because you backstabbed your best friend over something petty. Whatever...I'll play your game for now. I hope it was worth it. I hope you're happy in the end.*

He was still a bit uneasy. I had to loosen him up. He was still trying to scope me out.

"Hmm, yeah…I know how you feel. I haven't been feeling so good myself. I just got here about thirty minutes ago. I was staying home at first, but my mom picked me up on her lunch break. It's crazy how we both came in late."

"I know, right?"

"Yeah, she gave me some meds and rushed me over here. It sucks. It's not like I make bad grades or anything… I deserve a day or two off."

I rubbed my eyes a bit.

"Do my eyes look red to you?" I opened my eyes and leaned in for him to exam them. He came in closer.

"No…looks fine to me." That was the perfect chance to head butt him. I wish.

I pulled away from him.

"Good, then the stuff's working…so about the last couple of days. I didn't mean to be such a grouch. I was just aggravated. I think whatever I had made me a little cranky, soooo, if you're still willing, do you want to work on the follow up tonight? That's why I kept trying to call you last night. My bad…I was a real jerk."

"Yeah…about that."

I interrupted him by clearing my throat.

"You sure you're OK?"

I placed my hand on my throat and massaged my Adam's apple. "Yeah, yeah, I'm fine, just allergies." Out of the corner of my eye I noticed a bathroom over by the water fountains. It was time to carry out the next phase of the plan. I just had to get him in that bathroom.

"What were you saying?"

I walked over to the fountain and began to drink as he spoke to me. I wasn't paying him any attention though. I was just waiting for the moment to start my next move.

"So, what I was saying was about last night."

With water in my mouth I forced out another series of coughs.

"Are you choking!?"

He rushed over and began to hit the top of my back.

"You OK, Al?"

I hunched over and gasped for air. Water was everywhere on the floor; some had even made its way onto my uniform.

Perfect.

"Hey, Nader, can you run to the bathroom and get me some towels?"

"Sure, man."

He rushed over to the door.

"Hey, hold up. I might as well come with you. I look like an idiot standing out here soaking."

"Well, come on, then." He pushed the door open with his back and motioned for me to hurry.

I wobbled toward the bathroom. "I'm coming, I'm coming."

I had gotten him into the bathroom, so all I had to do now was wait for the right moment. I positioned myself by the sink and began to dry off.

"OK, Nader, first I need to dry off. We can worry about the floor later. It would look weird if I walked around with a stain on my pants. I'd be the laughing stock of the whole school until I graduated."

I picked up his nervous laugh.

As I continued to dry myself off, I purposely dropped a piece of paper towel and watched it in disappointment as it fell to the floor.

"Ugh. This sucks."

I stooped over and attempted to pick it up. "Man, I need to go on a diet. This is ridiculous. I need to lose some weight…can you get that for me?"

By now he had to be questioning himself, wondering if I really knew or not, but he didn't appear to be too sure. Now was the perfect time to get him while he was distracted. I just needed him to bend down so I could kick him in the jaw.

He began to bend over. *Just a little bit more, come on. The bells are going to be ringing any second now. Just a little bit more.*

"Wait…"

He looked at the bathroom clock and rose up.

"I got something I have to tell you…for the past couple of days, me and some friends have been working on a new track."

New friends? I thought to myself. "That's good. I'm glad you're still making music…"

"No…it's not like that. We made a track about you and we released it this morning. It's a diss track. You said that you just came to school not too long ago so you probably haven't heard about it yet."

"Are you serious?"

"Yeah, no joke. I can understand that you're mad, but I thought I'd at least give you a heads up…I can understand if we're not friends anymore."

"Why would you do something like that? Are you on drugs?"

"Look, I know it was stupid, but I said I'm sorry."

I could have killed him right there.

"You're sorry? Is that all you can say? The truth is I've been here all day! Do you know what it's like to have everyone against you? The day's not even over and I've had countless people hurl insults at me for no reason. I didn't do anything to them...I didn't do anything to anybody. But somewhere in your head, you thought it was OK to spread lies and slander my name? Was it worth it? All of this for a stupid CD...you satisfied now? You got what you wanted...so what's next? Did you even think that far?"

"Alex, it wasn't supposed to be this way. It wasn't suppose to go this far."

Then what happened? How do you plan something this big and not expect a big turnout?"

"You don't understand. Just give me a chance to explain."

"Why should I? Those kids out there didn't give me a chance to explain. Where's my second chance? I never got one. You took it away from me. Why should I treat you any different?"

"I know it's hard to believe, so just hear me out, OK? It's OK if you hate me. I don't even deserve to be your friend anymore. I'd totally understand if you never talk to me for the rest of your life. Just hear me out, OK? It wasn't supposed to be this way. You were right. I should have given it up a long time ago. It's just that I wanted that feeling again. It was good to be the center of attention. I just wanted to feel that again. All the rumors...that's what they were supposed to be. Just rumors. But the wrong people got involved with it."

"Wrong people?"

"Yeah, it was just supposed to come and go, but when word got around two others wanted to get in on it. I didn't exactly know how they wanted to help. I'd never seen you with them before, so I thought they would help with sound or something. I shouldn't have agreed; I realize that now, but when they were there, I couldn't just say I was recording something, so I was sort of forced into doing it. I know it's no excuse, but it's true. When they heard my verse, they would give me feedback, telling me it wasn't a real diss. So they threw in their two cents in between sessions. Eventually they joined in on the track. I didn't want it to end up like this."

The next question I wanted to ask was pointless. I already had my assumptions. But I wanted to test fate anyway. I was reluctant to ask but only because I was afraid to see if I was right.

"Who were the other two? What were their names?" I grit my teeth in anticipation and watched his mouth, as the names unraveled from his tongue.

"Rasheed and Sheldon."

"Are you serious? Are you serious?! Those two? What's wrong with you? I thought you were my friend. Are you trying to kill me?"

I'd been holding back my tears for the whole day, but I couldn't control them any longer. A river rushed from my eyes and poured from the side of my checks. I was just fed up. I was tired. I was angry. I was confused. I found myself caught in a torrent of my own emotions, and I just wanted out.

"What did I ever do to you, Nader? Ever since you came to this school, I've done nothing but look out for you. Is this how you return the favor? All of the good times we had, and this is your idea of just payment? Do you think this is fair? All for a stupid CD…"

"I'm sorry…"

"Sorry just doesn't cut it. How is that going to help anything? When I walk out of this bathroom, those kids will still hate me, my reputation will still be ruined, and you still won't be my friend. 'Sorry' won't change that. 'Sorry' doesn't change anything."

"Well, what can I do to make things right?"

"Nothing…even if you take the music down, they still heard it, and they will still talk about it. Even if you apologize in public, people will still remember. But, hey, you got what you wanted. Everyone loves you now. Good job. All you had to do was sell your soul. Hope it all works out for you. Good luck."

"You're not getting what I'm trying to say! It wasn't my fault!" he yelled from the top of his lungs. "I didn't want this to happen."

"And? It did. Maybe you're the one who doesn't get it. I know you didn't mean for it to happen, but it did. If you had been a true friend, you wouldn't have attempted this stunt in the first place. You need help. You sold out a friend for a profitless CD. All for a moment's fame.

"I…"

"There comes a point in your life when you're able to weigh the pros and cons of your decisions. You didn't think this through. You know…I originally brought you here because I wanted to jump you. But I thought to myself. 'What good would it bring?' There's no point to revenge. It wouldn't change anything. If anything it would bring me down to your level. All I can do from here is pick up the pieces and move on. I hope you have a good life."

I turned around as the bell rang and walked out the bathroom. Even though it was all over, I still found myself clenching my fists. I had to look deep inside of me to forgive him, but I knew it was something I had to do. It made no sense to be bitter. It would only hurt me in the end; I had enough on my plate already. Besides, bitterness only leads to self-destruction.

As I walked down the hall, I saw the building come alive once again. A few of the students saw me and began to call out insults. I ignored them and kept walking. Nader must have heard them, because he came out the bathroom shortly after me. I turned back as I heard the door open. For a moment I thought he was going to tell them to shut up, but all he did was walk the other way. *Figures.* His illusions of grandeur were more important than anything else he had in his life. It was stupid for me to think he would give it up. *Whatever.*

That day, after school, I bumped into Mr. Turner on the way out the door.

"I heard you wanted to talk to me? Something wrong?"

At this moment I had a chance to tell him. But the words never came out. It wasn't because I was afraid or anything, I just felt it was unnecessary. In my heart I felt there was no need. Maybe I was just indifferent to the whole situation. Looking back at it, I should have said something.

"Nothing. It's no big deal. I just had a question, but I found the answer."

"OK. You have a good day!"

"Yes, sir, you too."

The walk home was quiet. My senses were numb to everything besides my own thoughts. The cars bustling up and down the streets didn't bother me. The pedestrians beside me didn't matter. I was in my own little bubble. From now on what happened in the outside world was none of my concern.

"How's it going, baby?" my mom called out from the kitchen. She knew it was me. Jason must have come home early today.

"Fine," I told her as I marched up the stairs.

"Hold up. I haven't seen my baby the whole day, and you're just going to say 'fine' and walk off?"

I leaned against the railing of the stairs. "There."

"I had a long day. I just need to unwind for a bit. I'll be in my room if you need me."

As I walked away from the rail, I thought I heard her say something, I couldn't hear it, though. The sound of the shutting door overpowered her voice. First course of action was to search for the song. I had hoped that he would have the heart to at least take it down. I can understand if he didn't want to stand up to all those people, but taking down an mp3 would be easier. In a flash I pulled up our old music page and skimmed through the links.

Found it.

"Updated August 22, 2005, at 1:00 a.m., the song you've all been waiting for."

I should have known the song would still be up. At least now I could listen to it…I wasn't too sure I wanted to, but I had a deep-seated desire to know the truth. It had been bugging me since I talked with Mr. Turner. I didn't know if I made the right decision or not. I wanted to give him the benefit of the doubt, but look at where that got me. Maybe once I listened to this, it would bring some peace of mind.

I reached over to one of my side drawers and pulled out a pair of headphones.

"This is it," I whispered, as I moved my mouse above the play icon. I wanted to click it, but I had a moment of last-minute resistance. My finger stalled on top the clicker.

Did I really want to know what they'd said? Once I heard it, it wouldn't be like I could un-hear it. Once it was done, it was done. I would be better off if I didn't know. But then, it would eat at me until I knew the truth.

Even though I had second thoughts, I decided to click the mouse. My mind was telling me no, but every bone in my body was screaming otherwise.

I stared at my computer screen in silence, eyes fixated on the progress bar. I watched in anticipation as the numbers climbed higher and higher. The whining in the background from the computer proved that it was just as interested. It continued until, finally, it was stopped by a familiar voice…

Up first was Rasheed, followed by the others calling me every name in the book; hurling insults at me left and right, verbally condemning my whole person from head to toe. That was just the first minute of it. I was in shock for the other four. So I couldn't tell you what they said if you asked me. To be honest I couldn't tell you a single verse from the song. It was so surreal my mind couldn't process it all…to have someone go to such lengths for persecution was unfathomable. I came to my senses and snapped from my daze once the track ended in silence, but I didn't know exactly how to feel.

Should I make a track to get back at them?

No.

That would only lead to more drama. The odds were stacked against me. It would be best to keep quiet.

I heard a knock on my door.

"Dinner's ready, Al!"

I'm not hungry, Ma…I'll eat later when I have an appetite, OK?

"Alright baby, but don't get mad when your brothers eat it all up."

"It's OK. I'll find something."

"OK." I heard her footsteps dissipate as she walked from my door and back downstairs.

It was fine by me if I didn't eat…it wasn't like they were lying. It was the truth.

I sat up from my computer table still numb from it all. It was like a slow-working poison running through my veins and a gnawing sensation across my heart. The room was spinning, so I closed my eyes as I fell backward onto my bed. As I lay there, I felt it working its way throughout my body. My feet, my legs, my arms, and hands. It was slowly taking over; my pulse became faint. I could no longer feel my extremities, and my face had gone cold. The world around me grew darker, and I was losing the will to hold on. I could feel it traveling through my veins, bobbing and weaving through my interior, searching for its final resting point—my heart. As I realized this, I fought desperately to ward it off, but still, with every beat, it grew closer. I did all I could but my effort was in vain. I gripped the sheets in agony as I felt its cold hands encompass the very thing that I held dear. It was all I had left. I pleaded for it to stop, but still it squeezed. I gasped for air and pleaded for it to spare me, but all it did was laugh in delight as it grabbed it again. A jolt of electricity shot through my body as it laughed again. No matter what I said, it didn't stop. There was no use reasoning with my emotions. They had won. It squeezed again and I felt my heart seize. There was no use fighting it anymore. It would be better off this way.

The grip tightened until my heart beat no more.

To be honest I could care less. I just wanted all the pain to go away. I didn't care how or why. Maybe this was for the best. Now that it was finally over, I hoped they were happy.

CHAPTER 7

IT MEANS CLEANSING

The sound of my alarm clock vibrating on my dresser woke me. Even though I was awake, I still kept my eyes closed. Just a little bit longer. My plan to sleep came to no avail. I couldn't escape the sound. The constant buzzing eventually infiltrated my mind and lingered, waiting for me to take action. I sat up and tapped the snooze button and closed my eyes again, but it didn't work. No matter how hard I tried, I couldn't sink back into the depths of my subconscious. I didn't want to start the day. It would be better if I just laid here. Maybe I should fake sick.

No…

I would need a doctor's note for that to work so that wasn't going to fly, and I couldn't just skip school. It would just make things worse. Maybe I should just show up right before the bell instead of lounging around.

No…

I needed to switch out my books before the bell rang. Why should I care though? This was stupid. It was Tuesday.

The world of high school moved so fast the CD was probably old news by now. I shouldn't live my life in fear, and if anyone had something to say about it, I'd just show them who was boss. That's what I'd do.

And with that notion I sprang out of bed and began to get dressed. It was a good thought to begin with, but the closer I got to being done, the more reality started to sink in. It hadn't even been twenty-four hours yet. Of course they'd still remember. I'd be lying to myself to think otherwise. Sure, it would be nice to handle everyone who picked on me, but that would only cause more enemies. If anything I should go directly to the source, but getting involved with the three of them would only make the rumors true. I had no other options but to wait it out.

At school they showed no mercy. Virtually as soon as I walked through the door, I was greeted with insults. It was even worse than the first day. They taunted me wherever I went. It didn't matter where I would go, they always found me. I was mad, but at the same time, I was determined not to let it get to me. If I showed them it didn't faze me, they would move on.

People should have a heart. I shouldn't have had to do this anyway. It made no sense to hurt another human being for personal gratification. It made me wonder how people lived with themselves. But then again they didn't see it as wrong in the first place. Maybe when they were older they'd understand, but chances were they wouldn't.

When I got home, I felt the same as I had the day before, so I headed straight for my room.

"Alex!" my mother called from the kitchen. "Come eat. You're not going to have this luxury tomorrow. We have the mid-week service. So get it while it's hot."

I ignored her. I still wasn't very hungry. For lunch I had eaten from the vending machine, again. Two bags of chips and a drink. I just didn't have an appetite anymore. I was too focused on trying to stay alive out there. It was hard to eat when I had so much on my mind. I'd rather get through with this first. I could eat later.

I opened the door and yelled down the stairwell. "I'll eat it later! I have a lot of homework tonight. I'll get it when I'm done."

"OK, baby."

I lied. The only thing I planned on doing was sleeping the day away. At least I had peace in my dreams.

The next day wasn't too great either. More comments, more cruelty. I knew what was coming by now, but it still hurt the same, even if I had anticipated the blow. By the time I got home, I didn't want to hear anything. Three days was all I could handle. I felt like I was cursed by God. I must have done some unforgivable cardinal sin, and this was my punishment. I wished he would forgive me already. The burden was too much to bear.

"Boys, get dressed!" I heard my mother call out from across the hallway. "We're meeting your dad at church, so get ready to go! We're leaving in twenty minutes!"

I didn't want to go to church. It wasn't like everything bad would just magically stop because I went to church on a Wednesday…but I decided to go anyway because it was my mom's wishes.

It didn't take me long to get dressed. It was a mid-week service, so I didn't have to dress all fancy. Jeans and a t-shirt were good enough. Jason and Craig followed suit. We were dressed and ready to go in just under ten minutes; however, Mom was a different story.

When it came to church, we always had the same game plan every week. But, still, every week it didn't go as planned. Whether she had an epiphany at the last second and deemed the outfit she chose the day before was obsolete or she got caught up with one of her Sunday specials or picked the wrong make up, it was always something. Today she couldn't find her other earring. The three of us looked up at the ceiling as we heard her frantically searching for the missing piece. Just by the noise above me, I could paint what was going on with my mind. Right now she was probably rummaging through her jewelry boxes. Her next move would be to check the bathroom.

"It's always something..." Jason sighed, as he shook his head toward me. "Yeah, I know," I responded. "Hey, Mom! Just pick out a different pair!" As I said that, I heard the scrimmaging stop. Then I heard her footsteps migrate to the edge of the stairwell.

"Which ones?"

"What type of dress you wearing?"

"Blue!"

"Get some black ones, then!"

"OK!"

She was on the move again.

She said we were leaving in twenty minutes. We were pushing thirty now. "Same thing every week, Jay, and then she's gonna ask how we ended up late once we get to the car, ha-ha."

"I know, right? She'll get it one day."

"I hope so."

She came rushing down the stairs. "I'm ready, guys! Let's go! The car is already unlocked."

The door alarm sounded, and she was out the door.

"Come on! Let's go!"

"Chill out, woman, we're coming." Jason spoke for the three of us when he said that.

I love my mom. I really do…she's a pretty sane person when it comes to everyday issues, but if it involves us or church, she tends to go off the deep end.

"Get in the car! We're going to be late for church!"

She opened the latch to the van's side door and signaled for us to fall through.

"We don't have all day!"

The three of us rushed to get in the van. As soon as we were clear, she shut and locked the door. "Buckle up!" she yelled from outside. Her heels clacked as she shuffled her feet to the driver's seat. She sat down and pulled down the overhead mirror for a last minute makeup check.

"Mom…"

"Hey, you can't rush perfection."

She put away her compact and switched gears.

"Hope we don't end up too late."

Only in her world, twenty meant fifty…but it was OK. She had good intentions.

As we sped down the highway, Craig kept reminding her that she was going too fast. The speed limit was sixty, and she was going at least eighty. It would be something if she got a ticket in the Lord's name.

"You should slow down, Mom…God won't mind if we're a few minutes late. We'll get there when we get there."

"Yeah," Jay added, "You should seriously slow down before you get us killed…you'll be out three sons, and I don't think you'd take it that well."

She looked in the rearview mirror. "Hush, we'll be fine. Ya'll don't trust Mama?"

"Keep your eyes on the road, Mom…you're swerving into another lane."

She jerked the car back to the center lane.

"I'm sorry guys…we're almost there, so just deal with me a little longer, but ya'll, this here is pathetic. I don't know how we ended up this late. We need to get it together next time."

"What does she mean by 'We?'" I turned to Jason and whispered. "If I recall correctly, we were dressed at least thirty minutes before her."

"We need to come up with a game plan and stick with it," Mom said.

"Mom, you should pick out your outfit the night before…it'll save us a lot of time."

"I do! It's just that sometimes I like it on the hanger, but later on I figure out I don't like it on me."

"Try it on the night before then…"

"Well, it's just not that…sometimes there just isn't enough time to get ready."

"Well, start getting dressed earlier then…it's not that hard of a concept."

She scrunched her nose and gave me "The look" through the rearview mirror.

"Ale—"

"Focus on the road, Mom," Craig interrupted her again. "I don't want to die."

In the car the four of us went back and forth about whose fault it was that we were late. It was pretty much us against Mom. It was in good fun though. No one took it seriously. It was just how we interacted; hopefully she got the picture. Lack of extreme preparation for major events was reason number fifty-five on why I'm thankful for being a man.

We arrived at the doors of the church shortly after our little debate. From outside you could hear the music playing, so we really weren't that late. If we hurried we could still make praise and worship.

As we approached the entrance to the building, Mom gave us the usual pep talk.

"OK, when we get in there, I want you to say 'good evening' to everybody who greets you. Shake the men's hands and hug the women…and not a word from any of you when the message starts!"

"Mom, don't you think we're old enough to behave in church?" Jason said. "We come here at least twice a week. I'm sixteen and Al's fifteen…the only one you have to worry about is Craig. He's the youngest."

"Shhh quiet! When we walk through this door, not another word. Zip it!"

She looked back at us with her finger over lips and she opened the door to the sanctuary.

"We're not kids…you don't have to do that, you kno—"

"Sh!"

By the time we got in, the service was underway. We slipped into the audience and tried our best not to make a scene. The pastor had already begun to preach, but from the looks of it, we weren't too far behind.

"That's why in the midst of your trials and tribulations God is still there. When you look at Job, God allowed all those things to happen to him because he wanted to test him. God never left him. He was right there beside him throughout the whole ordeal. He lost his wife and all of his possessions, but he still trusted God; so in the end he was rewarded even more than he had been before because of his faith. Everyone is this room is dealing with something right now. Relationships, finances, health issues; some of us struggle with these every day, but how many people know my God is good? How many people know my God is a healer?"

The crowd was starting to get riled up. Various people in the audience stood up and lifted their hands to the sky, uttering in agreement.

"My God shall supply all my needs according to his riches and glory!"

"Amen," the crowd responded back.

"Whatever you're going through, you can count on him. He knows your pains. He knows your worries. He knows what you spend those long nights crying about. He knows what's on your mind. How many people know that the Bible says to cast all your cares on him? I know right now it may not look good. I know things don't seem to be going your way; they laugh at you, they persecute you. At your job, at your work place, at your home. Your kids don't listen. Your boss doesn't like you. You can't pay the rent. Things may not seem good, but how many people know that all things work for the greater good for those who love God? What things?"

"All things!" the crowd retorted.

"What things?"

"All things!"

"Now, how many of you know that greater is he that's in me than he that is in the world? Your problems are nothing to him. You know if he wanted to, he could just snap his fingers and everything would be perfect in your life…so why doesn't he do it? He does it to test us and to show us he's strong, so we can give him the glory. I don't know about ya'll, but when I was younger, I was arrogant. No one could tell me anything. Don't look at me like that, family. I wasn't always saved."

The crowd laughed.

"My parents used to tell me do this and that, take care of this and cut that, and don't talk to these people. Now I didn't want to hear that. I was eighteen. I was a grown man, at least in my own eyes. I had my own car, I had finished high school, didn't feel the need to go to college. I was even saving up for my first down payment on my house. I thought I knew everything, but I didn't. Now at the time, I didn't hang out with the best of people. All throughout my high school years, I used to hang out with my best friend Mike. I was stubborn but still a good kid. My parents knew that. On the other hand, they didn't approve of Mike. They never caught Mike in the act, but they knew something wasn't right about him…and they were right. I wanted to hang out with Mike because he was cool. So he did what the cool kids did. He spoke like the cool kids spoke. Eventually, I didn't just want to be around Mike. I wanted to be like Mike."

The crowd laughed again.

"Y'all are laughing, but I'm serious. I didn't want to be an imitator of God. I wanted to be an imitator of Mike. Mike wasn't a good person ya'll. Mike was sleeping with different women every week, his grades weren't good, he was involved with drugs, the list can go on and on, but still I looked up to him. That wasn't the type of friend I needed. That was my trial: to see if I would be able to get rid of him, but I never did. Fortunately for me God opened my eyes.

"One day Mike and I were on our way to a party. We were in his car and stopped at a red light, and this fool decides to light up some marijuana. Now ain't that something? The other people in the car didn't seem to mind, but I was about to pee myself once he started smoking it, so at the next red light, I asked to be let out the car. He thought I was just kidding, but I was serious. My father had been in jail for most of my life. I didn't want to make the same mistake as him. Prison wasn't where I saw myself ten years from then. I had aspirations. I wanted to be a businessman. I couldn't go out like that, so I left as soon as I could.

It was pretty late at night, so an officer stopped me on the side of the road and asked me where I was heading. Unfortunately for me he smelled weed on my person, and I was taken to jail. I told the officer to test me and that I wasn't high. I had just gotten out of a car with drugs in it. He didn't believe me. That night, when I was given my one phone call, I called my dad and told him what happened. He believed me. In fact, he knew Mike was on drugs. He said that he saw him in the back alley of a grocery store smoking something. He just wanted to see if I would make the right decision. I was a man after all. He told me he would pick me up in the morning, and that was it. He hung up on me.

That night was my first and only night in jail. I was mad at first, but now, as a man, I realize the moral of the story. The way I was with my parents was the way we tend to act with God. We act all high and mighty; we ignore the warning signs and the words of wisdom; we think we know it all and that we have a grasp on our situation; and then, when things backfire on us, we get angry when we shouldn't have been involved in the first place. The only reason God doesn't act against all of our problems is because he wants us to learn from them. I'm not saying the cause is your own fault, but in some cases it is. How is God going to deliver you from diabetes if you can't say no to an ice cream sundae? It's all about maturity, people. These trials we go through in life are so that we can grow stronger as a person and in him. Every night before I go to bed I pray for two things: to be a vessel and to grow more in him. How many people in here work out?"

A flock of hands showed up in the crowd.

"OK, so how many of ya'll know that to grow you got to do something. You gotta put in the work. When you go to the gym, you don't get results from liftin' them teeny tiny weights, do ya? No. You got to put just enough weight that you have to give it your all, but not more than you ca—

"Ya'll ain't hearing me."

He was marching left and right across the stage. The crowd was really starting to get fired up.

"Preach preacha!" A lady called out.

"In the Bible it says he will never give a man a burden more than he can bear. How many of ya'll got some burdens? Sho I do.

He raised his hand.

"Don't look at me like I'm crazy, ya'll got them too. I'm just the only one brave enough to put my hand up. But see, what I know is that while I have burdens, they are not more than I can bear. See, there's nothing the Lord can't do. I have my limits, but he has none. How many of ya'll know God is the ultimate spotter? When I feel the weight is getting too much and I'm about to go under, the Lord gives me just enough of a boost to get it off me. Look to your neighbor and say, 'The Lord is my strength.'"

"The Lord is my strength," the audience said.

"No matter what you're going through, no matter what situation you're facing, God will never leave you nor forsake you. Matter of fact, he will work it out in your favor. See this storm coming. Katrina. They announced it yesterday. Right now it's headed for Florida, but God's bigger than a hurricane. God's bigger than a tornado. God's bigger than anything we know. You think I'm worried if that thing comes here? I would praise God if it came here. Lord knows we need change here in the city. How many of ya'll know Katrina means *cleansing*? New Orleans needs a cleansing. Out of the whole United States, we are known for our crime rate, lack of education, and poverty levels. How many people know that darkness cannot give birth to light? How can we expect good things to come through New Orleans if all that it is known for is evil? I pray God shakes the foundation of this city. We need a Katrina. Bring on the cleansing. Hallelujah. Mark my words, that storm is going to hit us. That's prophetic. All our lives we've been praying for this city to change, and now it's going to happen. We want our kids to have a better life then we had. This is their chance because…how many of ya'll know that in death comes life? Once this city is destroyed, a new one will rise up. The *new* New Orleans. One where all the iniquity is washed away. One where your children can play safe at night, one where you don't have to worry if someone is going to break into your house at night, one where you don't have to worry if your son is in the wrong crowd, one where you don't have to worry if your daughter is going to find a good man, one where you don't have to worry which block it's safe on and which it's not. Bring on the cleansing! Hallelujah!"

He started to break down into tears.

"Bring on the cleansing, Lord. We need a new beginning.

"Right now, if there's anybody who needs a new church home, please come to the front. If you're in a backsliding state and you're ready to come back, please come to the front. There are new beginnings in Jesus. Hallelujah."

Some people in the crowd stood up and began to make their way to the altar. The crowd clapped and acknowledged them.

"I see you, my brother. I see you, my sister. Hallelujah. Don't give up on God, because he won't give up on you. Now some of you are sitting in your chairs right now thinking, *why I gotta go?* You think everyone is going to stare at you, judge you. But I'm here to tell you, it's not like that. All of us have been there before and there's a way back. I see you, my brother."

Another one stood up and came to the front.

"We're here for you. God just wants you to know it's OK. All those things you've done in the past, it's gone. He's forgiven you, now all you need to do is forgive yourself. I see you, my brother."

Another one rose up.

"Hallelujah. It's OK. We're not going to embarrass you. We just want to help you take it to the next level."

Two more came up.

"Praise Jesus. I'm done now…now, I just want to thank all of you up here for making this step of faith. I know

God is going to reward you for that. Now I'm going to pray over you all. I just want everyone to lift their hands in agreement.

"Father, I just want to say thank you. Thank you for bringing these people closer to you. Help them to walk with you, Lord. I don't know for what reasons they came up here, Lord, but you do. Help them to rise above all their problems on eagles wings, and show them your grace, Lord God. Show them how to live their life for you, O God. Direct their path and keep them in your favor, O Lord. We thank you for this, in Jesus's name."

And the church folk said, "Amen."

"And amen."

"Thank you all for your declaration of faith; if you follow the ushers in the back, we'd just like to have a word with you and get some of your personal information so we can see how you're doing and check up on you from time to time. Thank you."

He looked back at the crowd.

"Hallelujah. Isn't God good? Today we had six people come up. How many people know that the angels in heaven rejoice when a soul is saved, amen? I'm so glad that you came to fellowship with us today in the house of the Lord. I pray you all have a safe trip back home, and I hope to see you all Sunday."

"Go thy way and stay whole!"

After church we waited outside for Dad.

"Are ya'll going home with your daddy or me?" my mom asked.

"I'm riding home with Dad; he told me that you can't drive," Craig blurted out.

"Oh really, now?" Mom said.

She crossed her arms and looked past Craig. She spotted Dad. He was walking down the sidewalk with his briefcase in hand. He was wearing his olive-colored suit.

"Hey, how you doing, baby?"

He leaned in for a kiss, but instead of kissing her lips, he found himself tongue tied with her pointer finger.

"The kids are riding home with you tonight."

"They don't want to ride with you?"

"Apparently your youngest doesn't trust my driving skills."

"Well, you do tend to speed…"

Her smug look turned into a smile.

"I'll see you when I get home," Dad said. "Come on, ya'll."

As we walked down the sidewalk, Dad reached for Craig's hand, but he jerked it away.

"Man, I'm twelve. I'm not a baby anymore. Geez, Dad."

"My bad. It's just instinct."

When we got in the car, we buckled in while Dad adjusted his mirrors. Before we knew it, we were well on our way home. Dad had more experience when it came to driving. He knew how to drive buses, limos, all kinds of stuff…or that was what he told us. It didn't really matter, though; he still knew a thing or two about cars. Catch him anytime during his day off, and he'd be servicing one of our cars. I didn't know if that was a good thing or a bad thing. He was always a do-it-yourself kind of person. He was a hard worker, and he always liked to have fun. It was an admirable trait.

"So, which one of ya'll told your mama what I said about her driving?"

The silence of the car ride was obviously too much for him. It was a shame, I was enjoying the ride, but silence was something he wasn't too fond of.

"When we have our manly discussions, it stays between us. We are the men. *Comprende*? Do you want me to get in trouble or something?"

"She had it coming…it was the truth," Craig called out from the back seat. "I trust you because when you talk to us, you don't even look back. She turns back and everything. She's all over the place."

"That may be the case, but, son, you just can't tell women. You see how on TV when they ask you if they look fat or not. Always—and I mean *always*—just deflect the question. Be like the dress looks nice on you or something. Never directly, it's a lose-lose situation. If you say she does, she'll bother you about her weight twenty-four-seven, and if you say it doesn't, she'll think you're lying…I know you think I'm just talking, but you'll thank me when you're married."

"Sounds like you're talking from experience, Dad," I said.

"No comment."

"But wait, Mom's like a twig."

He lowered his head onto the steering wheel in defeat. "I know…"

Over the next couple of days at school less and less attention was heaped on me. Talk of the storm was beginning to surface until ultimately the school was closed. For the past few days Dad had been boarding up the windows and securing belongings. He wasn't sure if we should evacuate. The news said one thing, but in his heart he felt another. The storm had weakened once it hit Florida, but it was still coming our way. In a worst-case scenario, it could regain its strength in the Gulf and tear us up, he told me. I was still on the wall about it, but it wasn't my choice to make. He was the one watching the news, not me. Actually he was doing more than watching the news.

After we got back from church a couple of nights ago, I asked him what he thought about when the apostle preached his message. At first he didn't know how to take it, but then he came to the conclusion that if it's God's will, it will be done one way or another. He told me no man was bigger than God and, ultimately, what he sets out to do, he will do.

"If it hits, it hits; we just have to be on the right side of God when it happens, and we will be OK." That night we were in the study. I eventually went to bed, but he didn't. When he told me all of that, he had a fierce look on his face. He was good at hiding his emotions, but I could always tell how he felt.

Later on in the night, I sneaked downstairs to see what he was doing. The light was still on in the study, and he was deep in prayer. He was obviously more concerned than he let on to me. During the next couple of nights, this pattern continued. I wasn't against it. I was hoping my dad would make the right decision, but I was just hoping he would hurry up and make up his mind. The people on the news were already saying it had a chance. There was no need to risk it. I guess he just wanted to make sure.

I didn't mind evacuating. I didn't mind if we never saw our house again. I needed a fresh start. If Katrina was really sent by God, my only question was why it couldn't have come quicker.

Eventually Dad made the decision to evacuate. We spent the whole day boarding up the house and securing what we couldn't fit in the car. While we were doing that, Mom was trying to book us a hotel. Even though Katrina wasn't posed as a serious threat at the time, many people had the same notion. It took her several hours to find something, but eventually we found a place in Florida. It was settled. That was the twenty-sixth, and we were set to move out on the twenty-seventh.

"Say goodbye to the house, guys. This might be the last time we see it."

That was a comforting thing to say as we drove off, but I couldn't blame her. The last few days around here hadn't been too pleasant. With the news and everything, it would be hard not to get a little deterred. It seemed like, along with the winds and bad weather, it also brought stress. Constant worrying wasn't good for the soul, and it was starting to manifest itself in our personalities. I'd never seen Mom so down in my life. Dad seemed to be OK though. It didn't seem to bother him at all. He was always level headed in situations like this. In adversity he thrived, such as now. Even though we left at sunrise, we still found ourselves in gridlocked traffic. It took us at least two hours to get to New Orleans from where we lived. It was usually a twenty-minute drive. The two hours seemed like nothing compared to the rest of the trip; most of the time we were in bumper-to-bumper traffic. Normally, it took about six hours to get to Florida from where we lived, but three hours into the trip, we were still in Louisiana. Four hours, five, six, we were still there. Around seven we were just entering Alabama. Once the traffic eased up, we decided to find a motel to spend the night. I know Dad was tired from being on the road all day.

It was hard to find an opening, so we had to make do with what we had. It was only for a night anyway. During the car ride, we listened to the radio to keep us up to date, but not much was being said, just a lot of speculation and guest speakers giving their take on the matter. Some people were advising residents to stay; some advised them to get out as soon as possible. The theory was that if it sat long enough in the Gulf of Mexico, it would become a Category 5; but of course that was all speculation.

About halfway into the trip, my Dad turned the radio off. "It does us no good to worry," he told us. "God will protect his people." That was a comforting thought, but once we made it to the motel, we were all eager to know what was happening.

He grabbed the remote from the top of the TV and pointed it at the screen. Before he turned it on, he made us a deal.

"Now no matter what we see in the upcoming days, I don't what you to be worried. That's the only way I'll let ya'll watch. No worrying. Deal? No matter what is said, no crying, no sadness, none of that. All that matters is that we have one another."

The rest of us were on the beds staring at his silhouette as he talked. I didn't know how he did it. In my life I'd never seen him at a weak moment. While the rest of us had our doubts, he never faltered. He was always strong.

We all nodded in compliance, and he turned on the TV. The news was different from what we heard on the radio in the morning. Somewhere between the car ride and now, the state had issued a state of emergency. They were re-running evacuation plans and safety tips to ensure the safest trips possible. They even talked about running buses for people who couldn't make it out on their own. I eventually fell asleep, but I'm pretty sure they stayed up all night.

In the morning I was woken up by Mom making phone calls.

"Yeah, girl, you heard the news? What do you mean you're not leaving yet? You're going to wait it out? Don't stay at Grandma's house; it will flood...oh you're staying with some family upstate. Good luck. Stock up."

Apparently we still had family in the city. She was making sure they were OK. This went on all morning. Pretty soon everyone in the family exchanged numbers and locations so we would know where everyone was in case things got bad. On the news it said some of us wouldn't be able to return, so we were just preparing for the worst.

Dad was already up. He was reviewing the map to figure out where we needed to go next.

"When are we leaving, Dad? You saw the news last night. Traffic is going to be real heavy."

"It's still early, son. It's not even eight yet. Most people are just now getting on the road. The traffic is mostly in Louisiana, so we can take the time to breathe a little...the car is still packed. Once everyone is well rested, we can leave. Check in is at twelve and we have a room booked. We'll be OK."

"OK."

"Just relax, Al."

During the whole course of the storm, I tried to take Dad's advice, but it was almost impossible to do. Even he was shaken up at times. I remember the day the storm hit; we saw the live feed of the storm and what used to be New Orleans. It was torture to watch everything you've known be wiped away in one fell swoop. It was impossible not to let it hurt you. It just hit a spot. It's hard to explain. I didn't know things could get so bad.

Not everyone escaped Katrina. People were still left in the city; some even died. They were lucky if they died quickly. After the initial impact and the waters receded, the city was left in anarchy. One of the plans was to keep those who couldn't evacuate in the Superdome. It was a good effort, but in the end it backfired. There wasn't enough food, water, or protection. It was a poor living environment. It was virtually hell on Earth. On the news you would hear stories of people getting raped and killed; even in the dome it was bad. It even got so bad that people began to jump to their deaths to ease the suffering. It was depressing. Eventually it got to the point where we didn't turn on the news anymore. We didn't want to hear. We were convinced that our home was destroyed and all that was left was to pick up the pieces here. As much as I hated to say it, I missed our old home.

It was about three weeks till we heard anything about moving back into the city. We were uninterested. The people over here were nice, and we were already well adjusted Dad was offered a job at the post office, and Mom was with the government, so she could find a job anywhere. The only thing that stopped us from staying was when one of my mom's brothers returned and looked at our house.

It was only missing a few shingles, and the fence was torn down; so within the next week, we were home.

Looking back at it, Katrina didn't have that big of an impact on me, in a negative way at least. In the heat of the moment, it was a nightmare, but looking at it from another side, in a way I'm glad it happened. The apostle was right. The city was cleansed. Sure, it was a rough process, but on the whole we had a lot of stains to be removed in our lives. Katrina was just doing her job, and now that it was over, it was time to start all over again. This time I planned on doing things right.

CHAPTER 8

REVIVAL

Life was good. We had already been back for a couple weeks, and things were starting to fall back into shape around the city. We had already repaired most of the damage to our house. School was starting soon…tomorrow to be exact. I was kinda looking forward to it. Don't get me wrong; this was like a mini-vacation, but lying around in the house all day gets boring after awhile. I tried helping out around the house—cleaning, fixing, anything I could do to occupy my time. I even slimmed down a bit from working out. Point being I was ready to go back. Sitting on a couch just wasn't my style. Ever since we came back, I'd been wondering how everyone else fared.

But, hey, what can I say?

There really isn't much else to do on a Sunday afternoon. The church still hadn't re-opened, so our whole Sunday ritual was still in shambles. No more outings as well…most of the restaurants and movie theaters were still closed. Pretty much everything was off to a slow start.

Didn't bother me much though. These last couple of weeks had given me some much needed *me* time. You know that old saying, "There's peace in the eye of the storm"? It was something like that.

Before Katrina, everything was just coming at me at once. Bullies, self-esteem issues, grades, all of that; but now, even though we were still picking up the pieces, I felt like the time away gave me some clarity. I said it before, but I was honestly looking forward to going back, to see how things were. Things changed, people changed—hopefully for the better. But only time would tell. I was willing to give it another shot.

The night before school started, I had trouble sleeping. It was mainly because I had dreams of my first day. My slumber cocktail was a mix of anxiety and excitement. I didn't really know what to expect, so I was worried; but at the same time, it led to new possibilities. If I did things right, I could make up for lost time. I'd heard it over and over again that these years were supposed to be the best years of your life. I just wanted to make sure that happened.

And with that on my mind, I finally went to sleep.

At sunrise I was up. The light shone through my blinds and onto my eyelids, forcing me to start my day. I tried to go back to sleep but to no avail. My nerves were relentless. It was like the first day of school all over again. Actually, it was. It was the second first day of school. But there was more to it than that. Because of the area we lived in, my school was the first to open up. We barely received any damage, so now all the other same-sex schools in the area would be relocated to ours...which meant Jay would be around. On top of that, one middle school was going to be using the spare rooms around the facility…it just so happened that the school was the same one Craig went to.

Crazy, right?

For the first time in our family history, we were all going to the same school…so I could only wonder what the day would bring. Everything had to be perfect. I couldn't let what happened before the storm come against me now. It was enough to bear the burden alone, but if my family got involved, that would be the end of me.

Hope for the best but prepare for the worst.

My anxiety dissipated in the air, and I sighed. I was lying in bed still. Not that much time went by. Even after prepping myself for this day, I still had trouble putting my foot forward. I wanted to move, but at the same time, I didn't; too many "What ifs" were floating in my head, and they were starting to cloud my vision. Things were starting to be less clear than they once were. The thoughts that gave me serenity were now nothing but shadows in the darkness. They had no shape to them. I was starting to see what they really were. All of it was just wishful thinking. Why would my situation change? If it happened once, it could happen again. It wasn't like I had done anything wrong the first time. Some things were just meant to happen. You can't fight fate.

As I lay there, I heard footsteps from down the hall. I could tell it was Craig. He must have had his doubts too. He knocked on the door and peeped through the crack.

"You up?" he whispered.

I turned my head to the door. "Yeah…what's up?"

He walked over to my bedside and sat down on my bedspread.

"Nothing much…I just woke up and I can't go back to sleep."

In all honesty I didn't want to entertain him, but who was I to turn down my own blood? Nothing personal…it was just that I was still caught up in my own thoughts. As much as I wanted to focus on him, my sights were somewhere else—the ceiling fan to be exact.

After a long silence, the words reluctantly crawled out. "Oh…you nervous?"

"A little. How is it over there? Do you like it?"

In an instant the haze faded away. Somehow that question got through to me and really caused me to put my whole experience into perspective. I did have some bad times, but I also had good times. In life we all face ups and downs, and usually when we think back about the things that happened to us, we tend to focus more on the bad than the good. I knew I had been picked on and lied to, and my reputation had been tarnished, but when things were good, they were good. None of that was my fault, so why was I acting like it was me that was the problem? There was no use being afraid, so why was I holding this against myself? Fear is the world's deadliest poison.

"Did you like it or not…?"

"Craig, I don't know what to tell you. It's all about how you make it. School is just a place. It doesn't matter what grade you're in, it's just people. There's no use in being afraid."

"How was it for you, then? How did you make it?"

"Ha…so far it's been an interesting ride, to say the least."

"What do you mean?"

"So far I've come across friends, fakes, snakes, liars, bullies, and horrible teachers…"

"Oh…"

"Yeah…at times it was rough but, hey, I'm still standing."

"But you're cool, Al. Why would anyone mess with you?"

"I don't know, Craig. That's a good question. I've always wondered what makes people tick. I don't know why people do what they do, but it fascinates me. I personally think they did it to take out their emotions…but I don't know. Sometimes the reason people do things can get complicated. Like there was this one guy, Rasheed; he always used to go out of his way to mess with me. He had no reason to, but for some reason he always had to find a way to make my life miserable."

"So what did you do?"

"I tolerated it. I know, I know. Mom and Dad always told us to stand up for ourselves, yada, yada, yada, but things were complicated…and to an extent, I did stick up for myself. I guess, in the end, I was just afraid. Every time things would seem to get physical, I backed off because I was afraid of how things would end up. That's probably why I was an easy target. I didn't want conflict but, sometimes, you need to trouble the waters, Craig."

"Oh…is everything OK now?"

"It was only for a bit…do you remember Nader?"

"Yeah."

"Well, one day, after a scuffle or whatever, the principal basically made me the go-to guy for new students; that's how I met him. He was a good friend, but then he got caught up with the wrong crowd."

"Is that why you stopped talking to him?"

"Yeah…something like that. It's a long story. We fell out before the hurricane."

"Oh…are you going to try to talk to him when school starts up?"

"I dunno…it depends on how things turn out, Craig."

I knew I had no real reason to lie to him about the whole Nader situation, but it felt right to do so anyway. Craig was a natural worrier. I was just trying to look out for him. The last thing he needed to know about was how his cool big brother was the subject of a cruel joke for half of his sophomore year. He wouldn't know what to expect then. As much as I hated to do it, it was for his own good. I guess you have probably realized it by now: my conscience is always conflicted. I just have to remind myself that sometimes doing the wrong thing is right. Yeah…I'll just keep telling myself that.

You'd probably do the same thing too.

"So how are things now?"

"What do you mean?"

"Are you cool with everyone?"

"I don't know, Craig. It's going to be the first day. I haven't really talked to anyone since we evacuated. I hope nothing gets too chaotic. We were full with just the kids from my school alone; but with yours, plus Jay's and a couple of others, we're going to be packed. They probably have a system worked out so things run smoothly. Now if you'll excuse me, I have to get dressed."

I watched him as he got off the maroon spread and exited. I closed the door and began to shrug off the remaining sleep in my system. The sun helped with that. As I brushed the remaining crust from my eyes, the sunlight beamed though the blinds. It was hard not to be awake. Before I got dressed, I exhaled and did a big morning stretch. And with that I was ready to seize the day. I got my school uniform from where it had been hanging from the night before. I hadn't worn it in awhile. What was originally a deep forest green now resembled a lime color. I'd had the same uniform for about two years now. It was probably time to call Mom up for a replacement. I sat on the bed and put on the khakis, the steel-toed boots, the polo, and finished it off with the emblem. I was looking real good, if I do say so myself. It'd been awhile, almost too long. Maybe my excitement was getting the best of me.

After I got ready, I headed downstairs. Everyone was already up to an early start. From the stairwell, I could tell the festivities had already begun: pots rattling, the microwave churning, the news on full blast, and, of course, Mom's usual erratic footsteps. I could hear that clacking from a mile away. It came in handy when it came to keeping tabs on her though. I wasn't complaining.

As I continued to walk down the stairs, I got glimpses of the talk at the table. Mom was talking about her boss at work and how she could take his spot, if only they would give her the chance. She was putting more energy into that than her cooking, it seemed. We had all heard this story a million times by now.

All this time I could hear her pacing around the kitchen, but when I got toward the end of the steps she stopped. A squeaky floor board gave my position away.

She leaned from the kitchen and looked into the hallway.

"Alex...it's about time. Everyone's here but you. You're slipping up. You're usually the first one up. Craig even beat you...and you know he sleeps like a baby."

"I heard that..." he called out from behind the couch.

"I know, right? I'll bounce back. It's just takes some time getting used to going back to school. But you're already dressed. You're usually running around struggling to get out. Why the change of heart? You even have breakfast laid out for me...you OK?"

I took a seat and examined what she had laid out on my plate.

"Well, you know Mr. Brucestein?"

"Yeah...you talk about him like every other day."

"Well, I was checking my e-mail...excuse me..." She leaned over me and poured me a glass of orange juice.

"...and my boss sent one out about a test coming up for promotions. Your ability to climb the ranks is based solely on your test score and your experience, and, of course, openings."

"So you plan on beating out Mr. Brucestein for his spot? Wait. Isn't he your boss?"

"Supervisor. Big difference, baby."

"Oh...well, good luck to you, Mom."

I took a sip of my orange juice.

"What? Do you think I don't have a chance? I've been working there since before you were born. I have a pretty good shot...oh, and as for all of this, I figure the one thing he has me on is organization and time management. I'm good but not the best, so I figure if I keep the household in order and get to work on time from here on out everything will fall into place."

"I never said you didn't have a chance; I think you can do it. You have the drive. You've been preaching about that position forever. I'm just saying, now that the opportunity has arrived, now's not the time to doubt yourself...I mean, if you study hard for it you can get it. You already know how to work it from the back of your hand. All you need to do is put in the effort to beat him on the test. Do you think you can do it?"

"You're a smart kid, Al."

"You raised me. I'm just saying what you would have told me. You've given me so many pep talks, I thought I'd hit you with a little something real quick. You're lucky I didn't pull an Aunt J and get all in your face with it. Then you would have another thing coming."

"You're too much, Al!"

Even though she was laughing when she said that, she still looked discouraged. To be honest I wasn't too sure about Mom getting the promotion, but who was I to deter her from her dream? Enough of that goes on already. Too many people out here tell us what we can and cannot do, but in reality they don't know who we are, what's put in us. She'd wanted that position for God knew how long. Who was I to tell her no? She always told me I could do anything I put my mind to, so why shouldn't the same thing apply to her? Sometimes in life you just get that feeling that you're on Earth to do something big...you know, spectacular. When you find that thing, hold on tight and never let it go, because people will take it away from you. You have to do what you feel, because you only know what feels right. She told me those words; unfortunately, I haven't found what I want yet, but when I do find it, I don't intend on letting it go. Sometimes, we just need a taste of our own medicine. If we saw ourselves the way others saw us, we'd be surprised.

After she filled my glass, she put a piece of toast in her mouth and hustled toward the front door. I had the urge to stop her.

"Hey, Mom!"

"What, baby! You know I have to go." She called out to Jason. "Jay, you're in charge. Make sure your brothers make it to school on time. I'm counting on you."

"OK," he said. His voice bounced off the newspaper and down the hall into my mother's ear.

After she heard that, she turned around and resumed her fast pace walk.

"Mom!"

She was already out the door and inside her car. As she pulled out of the driveway, she rolled down her window. "I'm in a rush, baby. I'll talk to you later! Take care of Craig!" She rolled up the window and sped off right after she said that.

I had just wanted to tell her that she could make it…I hadn't meant to hurt her feelings. It was hard enough trying to find support in the real world. It shouldn't be hard to get it at home. I believed in her. I just hoped she believed in herself.

As she drove off, I watched her through the screen door. I could tell by the way she gripped the steering wheel that she was tense.

Dang, I'm sorry, Mom…

"Are you just going to sit there all day?" Jason said, as he came from the kitchen. He still had his same old khaki uniform on with his blue insignia. He already had his book sack on his shoulder and the house keys in his hand. "You ready?" He jingled his keys. Craig was behind him, fully dressed as well.

"I just need to get my book bag. Give me a sec."

"We'll be outside." As he passed me, he tilted his chin up and spoke out into the atmosphere. "You shouldn't be so hard on yourself. She knows you meant no harm. You think too hard, Al. Worrying only leads to more worrying. You're way too hard on yourself. Let it go, man."

"I know…"

His words hit me like a slap in the face but he only meant well. If anyone else had said those words, they would have fallen on deaf ears. A brother's touch can make the biggest difference.

"Now, stop standing around and get your bag."

"Ha, OK."

As abrasive as he is sometimes, I still know he has a heart. Call me crazy, but for some reason now, school didn't seem all that bad. I guess it was because I finally realized that I was in good hands.

On the way to school, Jason and Craig bombarded me with a series of questions about the school. More so Craig than Jay, but I could tell Jay was still curious.

"So what's going to happen when we get there, Al?" Craig was bouncing around with excitement.

"I don't know. We'll figure it out when we get there. I told you this is all new to me too. You know just as much as I do.

Craig seemed to be more excited than anxious now. I guess he was also pumped about the three of us being at the same school together. I was too. To be honest we all were. We were practically jogging to school. Poor Craig was trailing behind; he had always been small for his age. He made up for it in heart though.

"Is the campus nice?" he asked between his sporadic breaths.

"Yeah, it's cool. You'll see it when we get there. I really can't explain it. Besides, you've seen it countless times already, Craig…"

"Not the inside! I only got to see it a couple of times on half days!"

Jason turned around as he walked. "You'll see it when we get there. High school isn't as big of a deal as you think, Craig. You'll learn to hate it soon enough."

As he turned around, I noticed a sly grin across his face.

His statement carried some truth.

"You really think so, Jay?" Craig speculated.

"I dunno."

"Well, you should. You've been there for awhile now."

"I guess…"

Jason began to walk faster.

"Hey, slow down!" Craig said, but the more he begged, the faster Jay went.

"Mom said you have to walk with me today! You know I can't keep up! Slow down!" Craig persisted. He sprinted past me and chased Jay in hot pursuit. It wasn't long before they were in the backdrop ahead of me. Craig was still playing catch up, though. I could still hear him screaming, even back from where I was.

"Craig! Slow down!" I called out to him. It was no use though; he was too far ahead to hear me. Now I was the one dragging behind. As I watched them run off into the distance, Craig turned around and signaled for me to catch up and continued to chase after Jay.

"Craig! Wait up! Are ya'll just going to leave me behind!?"

Somehow we all ended up sprinting to school, one after another. Moments like these, although few in number, were probably the happiest moments of my life. In general any memory involving the three of us has a special place in my heart. It's sad in a way, though, to reflect on memories like these. In the present life has dragged us our separate ways. It was only when we were younger that I truly had the time to just be a brother with them. I wish I could have cherished the moments I had with them more when we were younger.

When we arrived at the school grounds, we were exhausted, but we were still laughing.

"The day hasn't even started yet and I'm beat," Craig said, as he collapsed to the ground. The whole campus outside the main area was virtually a huge field. He wiped the sweat off his brow and shielded his face from the sun with his hand.

"Can't we just lie here till school starts?"

Jason hovered over him and blocked the sun from his eyes.

"You know we can't do that. Nice try though…come on."

He dangled his hand over Craig in an attempt to get him up. "Come on." He shook his limp hand for emphasis, followed by a stare that broke though Craig's line of defense. Together they clasped hands, and Craig was lifted to his feet.

"You're no fun, Jay. We got time to spare."

Jason paid him no attention. Instead he turned to me. "So where do we go now? It'd be best if we get everything sorted out while we're early; the schools is going to be packed in a couple of minutes with the incoming students."

"Oh, you're right. That slipped my mind. I guess we should head over to the main office. That's where everyone should be."

Jay turned back and looked over his shoulder. "You heard that, Craig? Dust yourself off. You don't want to make a bad first impression."

When we made it to the front office, kids were already lined up and segregated off. A counselor approached us through the crowd of people, seeing as we were a set of new faces.

"How are you boys doing?"

"Fine," we all answered in synch.

"That's good to hear."

She pulled the dangling clip board out from her belt loop and skimmed through it meticulously.

"Now, let's see…you two look OK…but this one here seems a little too young to be with ya'll. He must be with the middle school assigned to be here with us. Name please"

"Craig," he muttered in a reserved manner.

She extended her hand out to him. "What's your name again sweetie?"

"Craig," he said proudly.

"Well, Craig, if you would follow me, I'll escort you to where your fellow classmates are. Your school will actually be intact, but just using our external facilities. I bet you have some old friends that are excited to see you. It's been awhile."

She grabbed his hand and they began to walk away.

"Oh, and as for you two, check-in for ya'll is over at the cafeteria. Your brother knows where to go. He has the uniform on, so just follow him; he should know the campus pretty well.

After she said that, she and Craig walked off. Craig looked back at us as he got farther and farther away. He looked kind of sad, poor kid. I could tell he really wanted to experience his first day with us, but things didn't quite turn out that way. "Maybe next time," I said to myself. At least he was in good hands. Now it was just me and Jay.

"Hey, Al, let's go."

"Right."

"Where's the cafeteria?"

"It's not too far from here. All we have to do is go through this building and make a left, and it'll be right in front of us.

"Cool. Lead the way."

"Of course…hey, do you think Craig's gonna be OK?"

"What do you mean?"

"Nothing. Never mind."

"You think too much, Al…he'll be fine. The only thing that changed for him is the campus. It's the same staff, same uniform, same everything. Even the students are the same. He's not going to get culture shock from being a couple miles away from his old school."

"I know but…never mind. You're right."

"Aren't I always?"

"No comment."

"What do you mean?"

"It's not like when we were young and you would lock me and Craig in the closet and chant 'Bloody Mary.'"

He smiled and shrugged his shoulders as he responded. "Hey, I offered ya'll money to do it. It's not like I forced you. I was fair about it, Al."

"Ha-ha, I was seven! Seven! You know what that can do to a seven-year-old mind? Poor Craig couldn't be anywhere by himself for a year after that. You call that ethical?"

"We were young. We did all kinds of crazy stuff back then. The three of us use to wrestle and throw each other off the top bunk, we had water balloon fights, and we even made adventure movies together. I was like nine when that all took place, Al…"

"Well, what about the time you said I was adopted?"

"Thirteen."

"And?"

"And it was funny. You're like the only black person in the universe with freckles."

"Whatever…black people don't even exist anywhere else in the universe. Either way you were still wrong for that. I tried a Google search for my real parents for like a week."

"Yeah, that was some good stuff; you do know I didn't mean it to hurt you. We were just three kids growing up. At least now we can look back and laugh at it."

"I have to admit it was pretty funny…hey, you know what I realized? How come when you were saying that, Mom and Dad didn't interv—"

"Hey, is that the cafeteria over there?"

"Does it even matter at this point? I need to get to the bottom of this!"

"We can discuss this later. Right now check-in is priority."

"Whatever."

"Jason always knows best."

"If you say so…"

After I said that, Jason jetted ahead of me toward the entrance of the cafeteria. I chose to stay behind. You know, it's good that he recognized it because I wouldn't have. The caf was nothing but a shell of its former glory. The once bleach-white walls had lost their shine. Now it resembled a khaki tan. Mildew was even visible branching out between the cracks of the more worn-down areas. Caution tape covered the right entrance…and handymen were still working on the roof. I never really had a sense of school spirit, but maybe this was something. I felt kinda bad for the school. It hadn't been that long and things were going well with the recovery, but still, to see it like this…something about seeing that just made me realize how small we really are.

"Hey, Al, are you coming or what? The lines are only going to get longer."

Jason's head was poking out from the side of the door. He was looking impatient. Apparently we weren't as early as we thought.

"Yeah…I'm coming."

He held the door for me as I walked inside.

"It took you long enough. Look at the line you landed us in."

"Would you rather be in class? They added an extra hour thirty to the school day to make up for lost time. So I'm not complaining."

As we were talking, another teacher approached us just as before, asking for our credentials and what not. Her task was to divide us into lines, depending on our general age and grade level. Lucky for us, since we were only one year apart at the time (my birthday's in August, his in October), we were placed in the same processing line; we were only to be separated once we reached the end.

Once we were directed to where we would be waiting, I began to see some of my past classmates...apparently some hadn't made it back. While some of us chose to rebuild where we left off, I assumed the others liked it better wherever they were now. I didn't see Nader. Maybe he had moved back. I hoped he'd made it out of the city in time. We had really fallen off these last couple of months. I had some time to think about what had happened during my down time, and I could honestly say I forgave him, but I chose not to forget. Wherever he was, I wished him the best of luck. Devan hadn't shown up yet either. I had nothing to say about him though. There were a lot of new faces around here now. I figured it was just going to be me and Jay for a while. I didn't mind though. We never really had much bonding time before.

"Hey, Al...aren't you going to introduce me to your friends? We've been here awhile now, and no one's even acknowledged you. Come on, Mr. Popular, show me the Rogers' legacy."

Question to the reader: Is it sad that I have no friends? By nature I've always been somewhat of a loner...and I've never had a problem with that. So, now, why did I feel so ashamed of it? In high school it's supposed to be about what clique you fit into. The jocks with the jocks, cheerleaders with the cheerleaders, nerds...but out of all of those, I didn't fit among any ranks. I never had. For as long as I could remember, it had always been just me.

When Jason said that to me, I hesitated to give him an answer; maybe it was because I was asking myself the same question. He honed in closer to see if I was paying attention, but he was met with my crystal gaze. He was looking straight into my eyes, but all he could see was two lifeless pupils.

"You OK, Al?"

"Yeah…it's just a touchy subject. I don't think my friends made it back after the storm."

"Sorry."

"Same…maybe they'll show up later. I'm sure they're happy wherever they are. They probably haven't called me because they got a new phone or something. You know FEMA is handing out money left and right." (*Or maybe I hadn't heard from my friends because they didn't even exist.*)

Sorry Jay…I hate to lie, but I had to do it. Why, you ask? Because as much as I hate to admit it, you're still that super-cool big brother, even though we're older. Look at you. You got everything together; with your grades, you're probably going to work for some big company in New York somewhere. I can't even manage to make a friend.

But I could never let him know that…

I quickly flashed a smile. "It's no big deal; we lost contact for a while, so it's not as bad as it seems."

"Well, not exactly…" Jason said, staring past me and pointing in the distance.

"What do you mean?"

"That guy over there is coming over here. He has a smile on his face. I'm pretty sure he's coming this way."

I turned around and looked among the crowd. Rasheed had spotted me and was on his way to personally welcome me back. I quickly snapped my head back and tried to remain calm. *Not now! Not now! Not now! Why can't things go right for a change? I don't need this right now. Not in front of Jay. God, can't you just let me win once?*

"Who is that, Al? Recognize him?"

"No."

"Well, he's coming this way."

"He's probably leaving to make a phone call."

"Why are you so uptight? Chill out. Do you have to pee or something? I'll hold your spot."

"Yeah, that's it. Hold my spot, OK? Be back in ten."

As I tried to make my escape, one voice out of the two hundred people in the room pierced my psyche. My whole body froze as I heard him roar from behind me, "What's up faggot?" In my gut I felt absolute dread. I knew deep down that I was about to be slung into the dark ages once again. I kept walking.

"Alex Rogers, answer when I call you, boy," he called out.

I didn't look back. I was afraid to look back. Not so much because of Rasheed; I feared Jason's reaction. I couldn't stand to see what he thought of me. It would kill me to see his initial reaction of him finding out that his younger brother was a loser…so I kept my back turned. I could hear Rasheed getting closer and closer. The bathroom was only a couple of steps away, now, but it wouldn't do me any good. That wouldn't change anything. The reality was that Rasheed was chasing me, and I was going to do next to nothing to stop him. Jason was going to see it, and I would have to live with myself after it was all over… so I stopped. There was no use running away. When he finally caught up to me, he grabbed my shoulder and turned me around. Couldn't he just let me be? I know I'd asked this question a lot in the past, but this was the first day of school. I'd been through a lot already. My parents could have died in the storm for all he knew; he had no empathy.

"What you running for?"

He had a fierce glare in his eyes. I never understood why he was so angry, but it didn't matter. I couldn't go down like this. In the story of Alex Rogers, I couldn't be remembered as some punk. I couldn't just be a victim as long as Jason was watching. It's crazy, the things people make you do. It's amazing how you can draw strength from a person.

"Last time I checked, I don't answer to that, and by the looks of it, you seem to be the faggot. You're always following me, going out of your way to say hi. Do you have the hots for me or something? Be honest, I won't judge you, but I don't swing that way, so can you please let me go to the bathroom now? Unless you want to follow me there too…and if you—"

In an instant he hit me in the nose, and my vision blurred as I felt my body drift toward the ground. Ha! I didn't even get the chance to finish my sentence…

That wasn't the brightest move I could have made, but it felt good. At least now, when I look back at it, win or lose, I did my best, and that was all that mattered, right?

As I continued to fall, I saw what I thought to be Jason rushing to the scene from my peripheral view. He was yelling something, but my head was ringing. I couldn't make out what he said, but I knew he wanted me to lay still. He came in and charged Rasheed without hesitation and tackled him onto the ground. The room was spinning, but I could tell that the other students encircled us and locked the three of us in a game of mortal combat. Jason was bigger than Rasheed, and it was obviously played out to his advantage. After Jay tackled him, most of Rasheed's fight was washed away. From that point on, Jason was just on top of him shouting profanities as he discharged his aggression against Rasheed's face.

I don't know how long he was hitting him before the teacher pulled him off. He was crying, and Rasheed was bleeding profusely from his lips and nose. I was bleeding too...you could feel the raw emotion in the air. No one knew quite how to react to the situation. Of all things that could happen on the first day, a fight had to break out within the first few hours. We were soon separated and sent to the principal's office. While we waited to be seen, Rasheed was sent over to the nurse. It was just me and Jay. An awkward silence set in. I was looking down at my blood-stained shirt. I couldn't look him in the face. I was too ashamed. I really didn't know what to say. If things were to go my way, we would have just sat there in silence, but Jason broke the silence.

"Why didn't you tell me?"

He was still wound up and he was sniffling between his words.

"I didn't know how to. I didn't know what you would have said. I was afraid…"

"Why?"

"I don't know. What did you want me to say: 'Hey, by the way, your little brother is a loser!' Is that how you would have welcomed your brother to your school?" I paused for a moment.

"It's just that you're so cool, I didn't want to come off as corny or lame. I thought all that stuff was behind me. I figured for a change people would have something else to look forward to besides beating me up."

"You think that matters, Al? I'm your big brother. You think it matters if you're popular or not? I don't care; I'd hang out with you either way. We're blood; nothing can change that. I'd go through that a thousand times more if I had to for you. I don't care how big they are. You're my brother, Al. And no one messes with you without having to mess with me. And I'm not embarrassed or ashamed either. You're far from lame; you're a pretty neat person, to be honest. I know I'm hard on you a lot, but I love you, Al, and no matter where we end up ten years down the road, I'll still love you. I know I'm not the best at showing it, but I just want you to know that I do and that will never change…OK?"

"Yeah…I understand."

"Do you really? I'm serious, Al. Don't try to go through your life trying to be someone you're not. You'll come up short in the end. All I ask from you is to be who you really are: nothing more, nothing less. Just be who you are. No matter what that comes out to be, I can't be mad at you because that's who you are. So if that just so happens to be what you are right now, I'm proud of you and I support you. I can't ask for more than what you got, kid."

I still wasn't looking at him. Not so much because of past emotions but because I couldn't see him cry for my sake. He'd put everything on the line for me back there, and I couldn't even be there for him. If he hadn't been there, then what would have happened? It would have probably been freshman year all over again. What was wrong with me? Why was I so weak? I hadn't wanted this for my brother's first day. I didn't wish this for mine either…so why had it happened?

I looked over at Jason from the corner of my eye. I was still hesitant to look at him. He had a gash over his left eye that he was clotting with his uniform. I must have overlooked it…

See, this is what I mean. It makes no sense to count on the good of people, because they will only let you down in the end. I thought Rasheed would have a heart and leave me be. I thought things would be different this time, but I was wrong. I'd never understand it, but I knew for a fact I was tired of being the victim.

Never again, I thought.

I just can't do it. I can't continue to live my life like this. I'm tired of being weak. God, I'm looking for change, because I can't take this anymore. You said that you would never give me more than I can handle, so don't you think I've had enough? Look at Jay over there. All of that for me…if I'd actually done something back there, none of this would have happened. Even if I had lost, at least I'd know I stood for something.

Never again.

I'm serious. Never again. Never again will I let anyone trample over me. I let this get too far, and to be honest I'm disappointed in myself that things are the way they are. It shouldn't be like this…if I wanted to, I could blame it on a lot of things, but ultimately it was me who let them get away with it. Yeah, they were in the wrong, but I let them walk away. So I'm the reason for all of this. That's why this will never happen again…thanks, Jay, for giving me a second chance. Your brother won't let you do down ever again. I'll make you proud one day. I think now I can finally look at you.

"Hey, Jay…thanks for sticking up for me back there. It means a lot."

As I said that, he smiled. I thought he was about to say something, but the new secretary called him in to be interviewed. I was sure everything would turn out fine. There were witnesses and everything. Rasheed couldn't lie either. He was at the infirmary getting looked at. When Jay got up, he turned back and looked at me with the same smile as before. I think that was his way of telling me that everything was going to be all right…I hoped so. Things could only go up from here.

It wasn't long before I got called in too, not to testify but to be sent home from school. Not only did we have a new secretary, but we also had a new principal. Mr. Turner would have heard our case, but the new guy simply didn't want to hear it. Bottom line was we were fighting, he said, and if you fight you were suspended, unless otherwise stated.

I didn't blame him…it was his first day at a new school as well. I knew he had enough on his plate already, but one thing he should have realized was that not everything is black and white. If he had heard us out, things would have been different. That was a given, but he chose the quickest solution. By the time I made it into the office, he told me our mom was on her way. I was hoping she wouldn't have to get involved. I guess I was being too optimistic. It was just that she didn't need this right now. On the first day of school, two of her sons got into a fight and now the baby was at school alone.

After he told us both that he'd called our mom, he told us to wait in the front office again. It made no sense; he didn't even get to see Rasheed. I don't even think he knew about Rasheed. If he didn't he probably thought we were in the wrong, because Rasheed was the one who was hurt. Maybe he'd let Mom speak to him. She was bound to be curious about what had happened. I just hoped she didn't go ballistic in front of everyone. Ugh… and she had to take off work. If he had just let us speak, things would have been settled by now. I looked over at Jay to see his take on the situation. I was a nervous wreck, twiddling my thumbs, moving around in my chair. I had even broken out into a cold sweat, but Jason was calm and sturdy, like a well-grounded fortress. His walls were impregnable.

He stayed like that till Mom came. That was the only thing that broke him from his trance. I didn't know exactly what they told her, but when she came to the scene, she rushed frantically through the office door. It didn't help that our faces were bruised. I was the first one she rushed to.

"What happened?"

"We're OK."

"I had a fight, Mom," Jay said.

"*We* had a fight," I added.

"Now what did I tell ya'll about fighting! Look at you now…you're all bruised and beat up." She stroked my left cheek, but I flinched back in pain.

"Ow! I'm fine."

"What happened?"

"Mom…"

"I deserve to know! It's the first day of school. Now I know my two boys weren't picking on some poor boy!"

"Mom…"

She lowered herself to eye level and gripped the side of my shoulders in both hands as she stared into my eyes. "What happened, Alex…?"

I was hesitant to speak. I was dumbfounded. I couldn't just look her in her eyes and tell her I had been bullied constantly for over a year. That would be too much. To be honest this whole situation was too much. It was all too much for a mother to bear.

"Not my Alex," she would say. "Not my baby." I could see it all happening right before my eyes. First, she'd get sad, then she'd be in denial, then angry…angry at a lot of things. Angry at me, herself, the boy…but she'd only reveal how upset she was that I never told her. That would only be for a while though. Then she'd start to blame herself, like she had done something wrong, like she was a bad parent or something. But it wasn't like that; it was all me.

I sat in silence as she questioned me. She sporadically asked me who, what, where, when, why, but I couldn't bring myself to respond. It looked bad on my part, I know, but I just couldn't bring myself to answer. They say that the truth will set you free, but in this situation it felt more like it was hindering me. I guess we can all say we have felt that way before at some time.

She gripped my shoulders tighter and asked again.

"Tell me, baby."

As I looked at her, I realized that I had no answer for her questions. Deep down I think she knew, but she never really said it. She wasn't angry or aggravated at me; she just wanted to hear my side of the story for her own peace, but that was something I couldn't give her.

Even if I wanted to, I couldn't. My mind had gone blank, and my perception had been altered. I really wanted to tell her, but I still couldn't bring myself to do it. I opened my mouth again to try once more; her pupils dilated and her muscles tensed in anticipation of the upcoming news. I could already feel the words resonating inside my gut; now I just had to bring it to the surface. So with one last-ditch effort, I tried to push the words out of my mouth. I was shocked though because the words that were spoken were not my own. They were Jay's.

"Mom…" he called out from the other side of the room. "We didn't start anything, I promise. We were standing in line, and Al was acting like he had to go to the bathroom, so I stayed to save his spot. Next thing you know, I see this random guy shouting and yelling in Al's direction, but Al ignored it…he didn't acknowledge the voice. The guy snapped, Mom…and went after Al for no reason. Al wasn't even doing anything. He never said a word to the person beforehand. Promise. He was with me the entire time. He just lashed out on Al. Al tried to defend himself, but the other guy was too strong…so I stepped in. He didn't know who I was, so I blindsided him when he wasn't looking. I know it was the wrong thing to do, but it was also something I had to do…I know Al would have done the same for me…because we're brothers."

Another save by Jason. It was amazing. The thing about Jay was that he always knew exactly what to say and when to say it. Even in the stickiest of situations, he always knew how to react. I'd never seen him stumped by anything in my whole life.

I think that was the answer Mom was looking for. By her facial expressions, I could tell that she was now at ease. She let go of me, stood up, and apologized to the secretary for making a scene. She also asked if she could see the principal. The secretary agreed and silently signaled her into the back room.

As I watched her walk through the door, I didn't know what to expect. I didn't know what they were talking about. It could have been anything. They could have been going over the terms of our expulsion, but we wouldn't know that. If I could have just put my ear to the door, I would have been satisfied, but the both of us were under heavy watch. All I could do was wait, and that was what I intended to do.

That was how that particular segment of my life ended. I didn't realize it at the time, but after she came out that door nothing in my life would ever be the same. In time everything would turn out the way it was supposed to be. Rasheed ended up being expelled, and I finally got the shot I desired to just live my life. Jason stayed with me for a couple more months, but then he ultimately decided to go back to his own school after construction was over. He said he wanted to graduate there. It was a better school, after all. I was OK with it, though. In those few months we spent together, I had learned a lot from him, and I understood that he had to go. It wasn't like I'd never see him again. It was sad, though, when he finally graduated. I remember when we were at his party and he announced that he was going to leave early for college to get a head start. I supported him, but it was ironic that just when we were starting to get close, he had to move away. I struggled with that thought for awhile, and he knew that. So I think that was why his last words meant what they did to me…

"Become legendary."

That was all he said. Then he drove off. Not another wave or honk. No goodbyes. Just those words; he left me with those two words to remember him. *Become legendary…* but how was I supposed to do that? I'm only human after all.